READ ALL ABOUT IT!

Getting into show business:

★   What you really need when it comes to looks, personality, and talent

★   How some stars found—or didn't find—their agents and managers . . . and how *you* can too!

★   Where and how to get training and experience

★   How NEW KIDS ON THE BLOCK came together

★   The stars tell: "The Worst Audition I Ever Had"

★   Stars who made it—and how they did it

Everything you need to know is here—plus a list of resources, including names and addresses of show-business unions, books, magazines, trade publications and more. Now it's your turn!

SO YOU WANT TO BE A STAR!

A·TEENAGER'S·GUIDE·TO· BREAKING·INTO·SHOW·BUSINESS·

RANDI REISFELD

Editorial Director of 16 Magazine

AN ARCHWAY PAPERBACK
Published by POCKET BOOKS

New York   London   Toronto   Sydney   Tokyo   Singapore

PHOTO CREDITS: New Kids On the Block (p. 10), photo by Robin Platzer; Fred Savage (p. 28), photo by Nader & Hashimoto; Paula Abdul (p. 42), photo by Scott Downie, Celebrity Photos; Neil Patrick Harris (p. 63), photo by Scott Downie; Alyssa Milano (p. 76), photo by John Paschal, Celebrity Photos; Staci Keanan (p. 97), photo by Janet Macoska; Tempestt Bledsoe (p. 111), photo by Janet Macoska; Kirk Cameron (p. 129), photo by Janet Gough, Celebrity Photos; Candace Cameron (p. 130), photo by Robin Platzer; Tiffany (p. 146), photo by Janet Macoska; Corey Haim (p. 164), photo by Retna Photo Agency; Debbie Gibson (p. 176) photo by Robin Platzer; Jason Hervey (p. 189), photo courtesy of Marcia Hervey; Johnny Depp (p. 201), photo by Scott Downie. COVER: photos of Neil Patrick Harris, Fred Savage and Debbie Gibson courtey of Star File; photos of Paula Abdul and Corey Haim courtesy of Retna Ltd.

AN ARCHWAY PAPERBACK *ORIGINAL*

An Archway Paperback published by
POCKET BOOKS, a division of Simon & Schuster Inc.
1230 Avenue of the Americas, New York, NY 10020

ISBN: 0-671-70192-4

First Archway Paperback printing September 1990

10 9 8 7 6 5 4 3 2

AN ARCHWAY PAPERBACK and colophon are registered trademarks of Simon & Schuster Inc.

Printed in the U.S.A.

IL 6+

*This book is dedicated to
every kid who ever dreamed
of being a star.
In my eyes, you're all stars.*

Acknowledgments

THANKS! For your time, insights and most of all, honesty:

Brian and Linda Bloom; DeeDee Bradley; Brandy, Dot and Mike Brown; Iris Burton; Barbara and Candace Cameron; Jill Charles; Carollyn DeVore; Sherry Eaker; Sandy Einstein; Maralyn Fisher; Helen Garrett; Ruth Hansen; Diane Hardin; Roqué and Sylvia Herring; Jason and Marsha Hervey; Janet Hirshenson; Linda Jack; Jane Jenkins; Staci Keanan and Jackie Sagorsky; Nola Leone; John Levey; Jeremy and Trude Licht; Meg Liberman; Vicki Light; Mark Locher and Harry Medved; Robert Marks; Kevin McDermott; Jeanne Niederlitz; Tommy Puett; Robert Richter; Edie Robb; Delores Robinson; Natalie Rosson; Judy Savage; Booh Schut; Eliot Sekular; Jerry Silverhardt; Pete Stenberg; Eileen Thompson; Tiffany; Paul Ventura; Donna and Teri Vivino; Wil and Debbie Wheaton.

And a special thanks to:

Pat MacDonald, Lisa Clancy; Desmond Hall, Katherine Hall, Russell Ryan, Hedy End, Chris DiNapoli, the staff of *16* magazine; my family, and friends.

Always, with love to Marvin, Scott, and Stefanie, for their patience, understanding and love.

Contents

CONTENTS

Introduction

"This is the best time in the world
to be a young performer."

(A consensus of opinion by
Hollywood starmakers)

As Editorial Director of *16*, the nation's first and foremost teen magazine, I've personally interviewed scores of young stars of television, movies, and rock 'n' roll. I've become friendly with many of them and their families and have been privileged to share in their daily lives, their triumphs, *and* their disappointments. I know how each of them really broke into show biz.

Over the years I've received countless letters from readers from cities big and small—the postmarks range from Nome, Alaska, to Flowery Branch, Georgia. Each letter is different, but all the writers confide a common dream; they all want to break into show biz—they all want to be stars.

I don't think there's a teenager alive who doesn't—secretly or not so secretly—dream of trading one-liners on a TV sitcom with Kirk Cameron, or having an onscreen adventure with Corey Haim, or sharing the rock stage with New Kids on the Block. For some the dream is vague, like winning the lottery, for others the desire to perform is burning.

Almost none of them has the foggiest idea how to

make that dream a reality. But the wait is over, for starting with this book, they will.

I've wanted to write this book for a long time. It gives me a chance to put it all together, to answer, I hope, all the questions a young would-be performer has about the world of show biz, about how to get there, and what to expect when you do. It also gives me the opportunity to share insights from Hollywood's starmakers, the agents, managers, casting directors, and others who work with young talent and who've guided the careers of the hottest young stars in the business. Most important, perhaps, this book gives some performers a place to recount their true stories and offer their personal advice.

There's good news and bad. There are more openings for teenagers in show biz today than ever before. There are also tough realities to face, rejection and rip-offs at every turn.

Some of what I have to say—and what the stars and starmakers have to say—some people won't like, especially those who are looking for a quick route to stardom. There isn't any. There's no such thing as an "overnight star," not even a young one. Some people will be discouraged—more, I hope, inspired.

I make no promises. I aim neither to dash dreams nor to raise false hopes, but instead, to give a clear picture of what the show-biz scene is really like for teens. I hope that what all young people who read this book get out of it is the feeling that whatever they ultimately decide to do—to pursue that show-biz dream, now, later, or not at all—is okay.

SO YOU WANT TO BE A STAR!

CHAPTER 1

A LITTLE SOUL-SEARCHING

So you want to be a star. Otherwise, you probably wouldn't be reading this book! I hope that, somewhere in the next fourteen chapters, you'll find out how to start making that dream come true. But before we get to the "how," let's deal with the "why."

Why do you want to get into show biz?

Is it because you want to be famous? To see your name flashing across a television screen, or two feet high on a movie marquee, or on the cover of a celebrity magazine? Maybe you already have a stage name all picked out!

Is it because you want to be rich? Does the lure of incredible wealth or being able to indulge your every whim fuel your fantasies?

Is it because you want to meet stars? Hanging out with your favorites wouldn't be too hard to take, would it?

Or is it because you just love performing, and you seem to have a talent for it. The idea of getting up onstage in front of hundreds of people thrills you. Knowing you can bring a character to life or make the

1

words of a song *real* is the coolest thing you can imagine. Hearing applause and feeling the love of an audience are just the icing on the cake. You don't simply want to perform—you have to!

RIGHT AND WRONG REASONS

Are there right and wrong reasons for wanting to get into show biz? Some experts think so. Some of Hollywood's most highly respected starmakers say that anything but the pure love of acting or singing is a wrong reason, that you shouldn't even think of pursuing a show-biz career for any other reason.

Hollywood agent Vicki Light feels that "to be successful, you must be passionate about acting. Otherwise, this business is too mean. It will mow you down." Those sentiments are echoed by agent Judy Savage: "The kids that get into this business have a need to do it, a drive to do it, it's like they're born to do it. My best advice is 'don't do this unless there's nothing else you *can* do.'"

But I won't tell you that. In my book there's only one wrong reason—and that's if someone else is pushing you. If you're not doing it for yourself, don't try.

Top Hollywood agent Booh Schut feels the same way. "If you're in it for the money, that's okay as long as the process is fun. But if your parents are in it for the money, that's the wrong reason. It's got to be something you want to do that benefits you in some way. Just like anything else, if it's in your guts, you should do it. But it should be part of your life, not the only thing you do."

SO YOU WANT TO BE A STAR!

Otherwise, there are no "wrong" reasons for wanting to reach for the stars. There's no reason not to try at least. Would it surprise you to learn that among the celebrities you know, some frankly did get into it because they liked the idea of being famous, of making tons of money, of meeting stars, of feeling loved? Corey Haim once admitted that he used to dream of seeing his face on the cover of *16* magazine; Johnny Depp loved making music, but he dropped it to act because he needed the money! Lots of young celebs candidly confess that they first got into show biz "because it seemed like fun."

But those aren't the reasons they stayed with it. Those aren't the reasons they made it to the top. Invariably, they became successful because they either started with, or developed, a real love for their craft. They felt a passion, a dedication, to hone whatever raw talent they had. They persevered in spite of lots of rejection and, sometimes, tremendous odds. They never gave up.

A FEW REALITY CHECKS

Whatever your reasons for wanting to be a star, you must know, right from the start, that show biz is *not* glamorous. It's especially not glamorous when you're trying to break in! It *is* a lot of hard work, long, tiring, sometimes *boring* hours. Mostly, it's spending money, not making it. Eighty-five percent of professional actors are unemployed on any given day, according to the Screen Actors Guild (SAG). It's a crazy lifestyle that means giving up things you take for granted, like being in school, hanging out with your friends, cruising the mall on Saturdays, just about all sports and after-school activities. If you're a young teenager, it means that your parents have to sacrifice, too. They have to give up their time, money, and lifestyle.

Because of that, Hollywood manager Diane Hardin advises, "If you can do something else, do it—show biz is too hard and too heartbreaking. Nobody that gets there, stays there all the time. The competition, the hours are brutal. It's not glamorous, it's very boring. You need dedication."

To break in and make it in show biz, you need to be totally dedicated, not just for a few weeks, or a few months, or even a few years. It takes a long time to break in. You need to love what you're doing and you need to keep on loving it! And you need to know that simply loving it is not enough. You've got to go out and try to make it happen.

Here's your next reality check. You can't succeed without your parents' help. There isn't a single performer I know, under the age of eighteen, who became successful without his or her parents behind him or her all the way. No two ways about it—parents play a mega-role in your getting any role! Your mom and dad are so key to your success in show biz that I've devoted a whole chapter to them—you may want to read it with them!

WHERE YOU LIVE

It may seem that all the stars live in Hollywood, or at least, close to Hollywood. And you don't. In fact, you may feel you live about as far from Los Angeles as anyone can get. Does this dash your dream for good?

SO YOU WANT TO BE A STAR!

There's no question that it helps to live within an hour's drive of Los Angeles, New York, Chicago, San Francisco, Orlando, Miami, Vancouver, Houston, or Dallas. They are considered media centers, and a lot of casting goes on there regularly. But even if you're nowhere near those places, you may still be closer than you think to people who can help. If you're truly determined, nothing will stop you, especially not a little mileage!

Is it ever possible to be discovered in your hometown? Well, no one's going to come knocking on the door of your house on Route 1 outside Smallville, Kansas, but on rare occasions, it does happen— usually because a movie company is on a talent search or because a movie is being shot in your area.

In those cases it may even be a plus for a teenager not to be from Los Angeles. Casting directors sometimes look for unknowns from different parts of the country to fill certain roles. Jane Jenkins and Janet Hirshenson, of The Casting Company in Los Angeles, explain, "A lot of the teenagers in Los Angeles have lost all their innocent kid charm. They get glib and jaded. We're always looking for that fresh, new, innocent-looking kid."

Director and former child actor Ron Howard scoured the country in search of kids for his movie *Parenthood.* He ended up with talented kids from Seattle, Chicago, and Gainesville, Florida! The producers of the TV show "The Mickey Mouse Club" found teens from all corners of the U.S.A. from Mobile, Alabama, to Denison, Texas, to star in that popular variety series.

If a big movie company does come to your neck of

the woods, you can't be sitting at home waiting to be discovered. You've got to be out there doing things, even if you're just active in your school's drama department (casting directors often call school drama or music teachers). Performing in community theater or being registered with a local agent are also good. The point is that, yes, there are opportunities for success even if you're nowhere near Hollywood. It's your job to be ready to seize any opportunity that comes a-knockin' and make the most of it.

STARS FROM "THE STICKS"

Not everyone's from L.A. Here's a brief list of stars you know, who came from places far from Hollywood.

Michael J. Fox, Burnaby, BC, Canada
Neil Patrick Harris ("Doogie Howser, M.D."), Ruidoso, New Mexico
Johnny Depp, Miramar, Florida
Richard Grieco, Watertown, New York
Annabeth Gish, Cedar Falls, Iowa
Winona Ryder, Petaluma, California
Heather Langencamp ("Just the Ten of Us"), Tulsa, Oklahoma
Demi Moore, Roswell, New Mexico
Courteney Cox, Birmingham, Alabama
Monique Lanier ("Life Goes On"), Ogden, Utah
Thomas Wilson Brown (Honey, I Shrunk the Kids), Santa Fe, New Mexico

SO YOU WANT TO BE A STAR!

Judd Nelson, Portland, Maine

Robert Rusler ("The Outsiders"), Ft. Wayne, Indiana

New Kids Donnie, Danny, Jon and Jordan, Dorchester, Massachusetts

New Kid Joe McIntyre, Jamaica Plain, Massachusetts

THE DREADED R *WORD*

Before you turn the page and start learning the inside secrets of how to get going, there's one more thing to think about seriously. That's the *R* word—as in *Rejection!* How well you handle it may determine if you ever get started or not! For rejection and a career in show biz go hand-in-hand. You will be rejected pursuing this career more than any other. You'll be turned away each and every step of the way. If you let it stop you, show biz is not for you! If you let rejection "eat away" at you, give it up before you go any further!

Agent Helen Garrett puts it this way: "You need a good self-image and a lot of support from your family, assuring you you're great, because rejection, rejection, rejection is the name of the game in this business."

Aspiring actors will go on from twenty to sixty-five auditions before landing *one single job.* Singers may have to distribute hundreds of demo tapes before even getting a single response—that's the average. It's even harder for girls to break in than boys.

If you can accept this, if you can go out on auditions, do your best, then go home and forget about it, you're on the right track. In "All About Auditions," Chapter 6, you'll see that there's not a single star you know who hasn't lost out on more roles than he or she has gotten. You'll be surprised to find out who was up for what role and didn't get it!

THE NEW KIDS ON THE BLOCK STORY!

Is there a kid on any block in any town who hasn't heard of Donnie, Danny, Jordan, Jonathan, and Joe —the New Kids on the Block? They're the most famous band there is right now! Yet these five boys from Boston started out just like you, with no connections, far from Hollywood, and with only the vaguest idea of what show biz was all about. They didn't "happen" overnight. They worked hard and had many doors slammed in their faces before stardom hit.

The New Kids story is that of the "dream open-audition," the kind of audition any kid on any block might fantasize about. It started back in 1984 when singer and producer Maurice Starr, along with talent manager Mary Alford, decided to create a pop-rap group. Maurice had had success with a band of black teens called New Edition, and he wanted to duplicate that success using a group of five musically talented and appealing white teens. He and Mary put out the word that open auditions were being held throughout the summer of 1984 in Boston.

NEW KIDS ON THE BLOCK

SO YOU WANT TO BE A STAR!

Many young hopefuls turned out. The first one signed was Donnie Wahlberg, of Dorchester, Massachusetts. Maurice was impressed with Donnie's dancing ability and his natural abilities as a leader. He also liked Donnie's younger brother Mark, and for a short time he, too, was a New Kid.

Maurice and Mary were having trouble finding other Kids, though, and they asked Donnie if he had any talented friends. It was Donnie who brought fellow street dancer Danny Wood aboard. Then he introduced singers Jon and Jordan Knight, whom he'd known since grade school, to them.

Little Joe McIntyre joined a bit later, also through an audition!

The fivesome worked every day after school and on weekends, learning the music and the dances Maurice and his brother Sonni taught them. Keeping up with schoolwork, a rigid rehearsal schedule, and their after-school jobs was a grind, but the Kids were dedicated.

To gain experience they started playing small clubs in and around Boston. They met with little success. At one memorable gig, they were actually booed off the stage! Jonathan admits, "There was a lot of disappointment in those early days." There were a lot of ups and downs. Donnie adds, "When we did a concert and it went well, we'd feel like heroes for that one night onstage. Then the next day we'd wake up, get on the subway, go back to school, like normal kids."

Naturally, the goal was to get New Kids a recording contract, and Maurice used his music industry contacts. He sent demo tapes to record labels, but in the beginning he got no responses. In January 1986,

Columbia Records decided to take a chance on the Kids and, in April of that year, released their first single, "Be My Girl." To put it bluntly, it bombed. So did the LP from which it came, *New Kids on the Block*. It wasn't from lack of trying on the boys' part. They gamely set about on the concert trail in support of their album, enduring ten-hour bus rides between gigs.

Luckily, New Kids got a second chance, and in 1988 they released their *Hangin' Tough* album. This, too, might've died if it weren't for two twists of fate. A savvy deejay saw the Kids on video and knew that Joe McIntyre had the makings of a teen idol. He began playing their single, "Please Don't Go Girl" on his station—other radio stations quickly followed.

The Tiffany Connection

But the Kids' biggest break came because of pop star Tiffany, who picks up the story:

"I had the same booking agents as New Kids (Jerry and John Ade of Famous Artists). And they promised them—without even asking me or my manager—that they could do a show with me. I was going to be performing in Westbury, Long Island, and Jerry called me and said, 'I have this act, I want them to audition for you.' But he didn't mention that he already promised them they would go onstage with me that night!

"I was having dinner with my manager [George Tobin], my best friend, and my aunt. We were sitting there in this really small room when the New Kids came in. And they started singing and doing all their choreography right in front of us. And I remembered when *I* used to do that, auditioning in front of people who were, like, on the phone and eating. When I was finished, they'd say, 'That was good,' but I'd think, 'How do you even know? You weren't even paying attention.'

"So I watched them and I looked at my girlfriend. Of course, being girls, we're looking and thinking, 'Which one's the cutest?' So we'd look at each other and put our food down—George was still eating and I was really embarrassed.

"The New Kids did their number and they went out and George said, 'Well, what do you think?' Then the agent came in and confessed that he'd already promised them they could be on the bill that night. George was upset, but I said, 'Look it's a positive, good thing. The guys are really good-looking and they sound great. I like their music. Besides, my crowd is mostly girls, anyway, and those girls are gonna go screaming for five gorgeous-looking guys!'

"So we put them on, and when I was backstage, listening to the screams, I just said, 'Yeah!' "

New Kids: One By One

New Kid Donnie Wahlberg

"I've always wanted to be famous," New Kid Donnie admits. One of nine from a hardworking Boston family, Donnie did his best to make sure *he* was the center of attention at all times.

As a young teen, he had a reputation as a tough guy, but he was one young tough who "secretly dreamed of being a rock or rap star." Donnie didn't go to music classes to make that dream come true—the streets were his school. Mimicking his black friends, Donnie taught himself rap routines and composed rap rhymes. He was best known in his neighborhood for a mean impression of his idol, Michael Jackson.

Along with his best friend Danny Wood and some other musical guys, he performed at local parties. Donnie details, "We loved it, especially all the attention we got from girls!"

In 1984 a friend urged Donnie to try out for New Kids. "To me, the audition was just something to do," Donnie admits. He never thought it would amount to anything and he almost didn't go. "I didn't think I was a good enough singer," he confessed. The friend kept pushing, however, and Donnie rapped and danced and did his best. When he was accepted as a New Kid, he thought immediately of his old friend Danny.

Donnie's advice for would-be stars—"Never give up. Be patient and fulfill your goals."

New Kid Danny Wood

Danny's also from a big Boston family—he's one of six. None of the Wood clan had any connections to show biz—higher education was the main goal for all the Wood kids. Danny was a straight-A student who'd won a scholarship to Boston University just before New Kids came along!

In spite of his good grades, Danny spent a lot of time on the streets, where, influenced by school friends, he became a master breakdancer. He admits,

14

however, that he didn't really have any definite ambitions before he joined New Kids.

Danny finds auditions "scary," and it took him a while before he agreed to try out. Being accepted posed a major problem for Danny—it meant giving up his scholarship to college. His parents were worried that the group would go nowhere, and at first they weren't sure he should postpone college. But Danny decided to follow the dream. Clearly it all worked out!

His advice to you—"Stick with it, don't give up!"

New Kids Jon and Jordan Knight

Though from a nonshow-biz family, Jon and Jordan Knight were brought up around music—lots of it. Their grandparents could read music; their dad played the piano; their mom played the accordion. Jon and Jordan sang all the time; they were in their school's chorus and got a good deal of solid musical training in their church choir. A talented choirmaster took special interest in the brothers and helped them develop their young voices.

In spite of their backgrounds, however, neither Knight gave much thought to going professional. "I always just wanted to sing, but I didn't really want to be famous," Jordan once confessed. "I was afraid guys would be jealous and hate me. So I didn't let myself dream of being a pop star."

His shy older brother Jon, plagued all his young life by stage fright, felt the same way. It wasn't until Donnie Wahlberg came a-callin' and convinced Jon and Jordan to try out for New Kids that either boy gave a thought to recording. Even after they joined, Jordan still had second thoughts: "When I first joined, I still wasn't sure it was the right thing to do. It was only after a year of being with the group that I knew I *really* wanted to be part of it. It's a once-in-a-lifetime opportunity."

Once their mom was convinced that Maurice Starr was legit, she threw her support behind her sons. "Mom encouraged us," say Jon and Jordan. "She told us we could do anything we wanted to."

Jordan acknowledges that it hasn't all been totally cool with the group. "Having our first song flop was the biggest disappointment of my life," he admits. But he has always followed the advice he gives to you— "Strive to be number one at whatever you do."

New Kid Joe McIntyre

The youngest member of the band always had the biggest dreams. "I wanted to be a singing star, I wanted to be a hit at the Apollo," Joe says, referring to New York City's famous soul theater. Joe, too, is from a large family (he's one of nine), and every one of the McIntyres is into entertaining. "They all sang and acted," Joe relates. His older sister Judith was on a TV soap opera, and his dad once did a TV commercial in support of Massachusetts Governor Michael Dukakis.

When he was six, Joe was "bitten by the acting bug," and he began performing in the Neighborhood Children's Theater of Boston. Joe once played the lead in *Oliver,* and his whole family stood around him singing the opening number. Naturally, when New

Kids came into Joe's life, all the McIntyres supported his decision to join.

In the beginning, being in the group was stressful for Joe. Not only was he the only member to have to take his schoolwork on the road—he joined at thirteen—but also he sometimes wished he could "just go home after school, play football with my friends and have a regular life." Those feelings didn't last long once the group got into its hit-making groove. Joe unabashedly admits he loves not only recording and performing with the group, but also he gets a kick out of how famous they are, too.

Joe's advice to would-be rock stars—"Keep practicing!"

CHAPTER 2

(YOU GOT IT)
THE RIGHT STUFF

If you're like most young people, you often wonder, "Do I have what it takes to make it in show biz?"

YOUR LOOKS

Does it seem to you that all stars are great looking? Look again. Granted, some are pretty, but most are pretty ordinary! In fact, "ordinary" is exactly what a lot of agents and casting directors are looking for right now. It wasn't always that way. In past years starmakers did go after the most gorgeous, handsome, and beautiful kids, but things have changed and the look in demand now is the "natural boy- or girl-next-door."

That said, let's qualify it. Although beauty is in the eye of the beholder, it doesn't hurt to be gorgeous! But it isn't necessary. For every Alyssa Milano (who, by the way, doesn't think she's gorgeous), there's a Ricki Lake, whose unusual looks haven't hurt *her* career. For every Robin Givens, there's a Whoopi Goldberg. For every glamorous Christie Brinkley, there are superstars like Bette Midler, Meryl Streep, Debbie Gibson, Tiffany, and Madonna who have unique looks, but by normal standards are not model gorgeous. Roseanne Barr, TV's biggest star, certainly defies the traditional concept of beauty!

Being beautiful isn't necessary onstage or in the rock or dance world, areas of show biz where looks count least.

There are some stars who say being considered really gorgeous has even worked against them. Actor Brian Bloom tells the story of the audition he worked really hard preparing for, staying up the whole night before it to get ready. But he never got a chance to try out because as soon as he walked in the door, he was told, "Oh, you're too good-looking, forget it." Richard Grieco recounts similar episodes.

No one's implying that you shouldn't look your best. Proper diet and exercise are important no matter what you do. Besides, when you feel you look good, you feel good about yourself. And that's a key to success!

In commercials casting is changing, too. Once, only wholesome-looking cutie-pies were hired, but now that's changing. In fact, it may be easier to get a jump start in commercials (which is where most kids get started) if you're not gorgeous. As Hollywood agent Helen Garrett explains, "Often, what they're looking for is the average teen, so that the viewer may think, 'Oh, she looks just like our niece, or daughter, or granddaughter.' And they'll be more disposed to buy the product in the commercial."

Every agent, manager, casting director, and producer in show biz confirms that there are openings for every type—skinny, nerdy, intellectual, chubby, short, tall, Hispanic, Black, Caucasian, Asian, street-wise, you name it!

Therein, however, lies the trick. Though you don't need knock-out looks to break into show biz, you do have to have "a look." There has to be something that's unique about you. Everyone has his or her own character, you need to identify yours. Best way to do that is to watch TV, only not the way you usually do. Instead of simply enjoying the story, study the characters on each show carefully and try to determine which of them seems the most like you. Think about where you'd fit in. For in nine out of ten shows, the different characters represent different "types."

The old TV sitcom (now in reruns) "Facts of Life" is a good example. It starred four girls, each very obviously a different type: Blair (Lisa Whelchel) was the blond, blue-eyed beauty; Jo (Nancy McKeon) was the streetwise, hip one; Natalie (Mindy Cohn) was the funny, chubby one; while Tootie was the wise, warm, ethnic one. The same exact "formula" applies to the long-running sitcom, "Head of the Class." There's a hip one (Brian Robbins), a handsome preppy (Tony O'Dell), a nerd (Dan Frischman), a fat one (Dan Schneider), a stunner (Robin Givens), a blond (Lara Piper), etc., etc., etc.

Where does your look fit in? Check out not only the stars of each show, or movie, but also cast a critical eye on the supporting players. In most cases, especially among teenagers, the actors who portray school-mates and friends are hired because they look real, natural, and believable.

The most important thing to understand about looks in this business is something that's totally beyond your control. It's simply this—*you must fit the part.* Whenever a role is written—whether it's in a TV show, a movie, or a commercial—the writer, producer, and director have a vision of what that character should look like. The actors who are eventually cast usually conform to that vision. Take "The Wonder Years," for example. The character Kevin, coming of age in the 1960s, must seem innocent and curious— he must also be lovable since he *is,* after all, the lead! Doesn't wholesome, saucer-eyed cutie-pie Fred Savage fit that description to a *T?* Kevin's best friend Paul is the classic nerd; actor Josh Saviano, whose offbeat looks can be played up to fit that description, was cast in the role. Jason Hervey's funny face helped win him the part of the older brother, wisecracking Wayne, while winsomely pretty Olivia D'Abo is the perfect match as sister, Karen, a long-haired hippie of that era. Sweetly pretty, but not gorgeous and intimidating, Danica McKellar fits the part of the girl-next-door.

If you don't fit into any particular look, don't despair. For looks, as you'll see soon, really mean very little without personality, training, determination, perseverance, and talent. If you've got the other ingredients, a look can be developed. Not all the kids in show biz started out looking the way you see them now. All had some kind of professional advice along the way. You'll get there!

Some general tips to think about: Have you ever seen a teen on TV with crooked teeth? With braces? Not too often. Reality has its limits! You probably will not break in until after your teeth have been straightened. Yes, there are such things as clear braces, or braces the color of your teeth. (Jordan Knight wears these.) If it's important to you, check with your orthodontist and, of course, with your mom and dad (the clear ones may be more expensive).

It helps to look younger than you are. As a general rule, it also helps to be small for your age. Meg Liberman, of Liberman/Hirschfeld Casting, who casts "The Wonder Years," reveals, "We're always looking for girls who are small and young looking to play opposite Fred Savage who's short and looks younger than his age."

As a teenager or preteen your looks are constantly changing, so don't obsess about them. With proper training you can create a look that's all your own.

YOUR PERSONALITY

Is there a specific type of personality that it takes to be a star? While there are no hard-and-fast rules, some traits may get you started sooner.

It helps to be outgoing, as long as you're not phony about it. Personality will help attract the interest of an agent or manager—and in the world of TV and movies you will eventually need an agent to get most acting jobs. Even in the theater, where you don't necessarily need representation, or in the music world, you still need to impress people to get started.

What does that mean exactly? It means that when you walk into an agent's office or a casting director's studio, you have a very short time to make an impression—and you have to make that impression on people who may have seen two hundred teens before you that same day! Suppose you're asked, "How are you?" You've got to want to say more than "fine." Most young performers are the kind who'd naturally answer, "I'm great today, and you want to know why? My softball team just won our first game!" Or they'd say, "I'm in a really great mood because tomorrow's my birthday and I've got a great party planned." You have to make a roomful of adults want to get to know you better. That can be scary, especially for a young person.

Ruth Hansen of the Harry Gold Agency advises, "Outgoing is important, but there's got to be a warmth to your personality, it's got to be you." Manager Diane Hardin elaborates, "In my experience, the personality type that succeeds is someone who's very determined and generally outgoing. I tell my clients, 'Be comfortable with yourself and make that interviewer comfortable.'"

Never try to change your personality, however, or copy anyone to fit what you think someone else wants you to be. "Your strength as a performer is your uniqueness as a person," says top drama coach Kevin McDermott, who operates Center Stage L.A. Besides, there are major exceptions to every rule. Every agent or casting director knows at least one star who doesn't fit the profile of "outgoing, bubbly, sparkly." "If someone's truly, truly talented," says Diane Hardin, "it doesn't matter what the personality is. He or she will work."

The experts hasten to add that only if you're going up for a commercial is an outgoing personality really critical. If it's a movie or TV role you're interviewing for, it's okay to be less bubbly. And if it's stage work you're auditioning for, or a musical gig, your talent speaks for you—not your personality.

What if you're downright bashful? Admittedly, shy types are going to have a hard time breaking into any aspect of show biz. Some talent agents come right out and say, "If you're shy and thin-skinned, you don't belong in this business, because people can be cruel."

I won't say that, because I don't think it's categorically true. I agree, instead, with agent Natalie Rosson, whose experience has taught her that "the quiet ones are often the most gifted." There are different kinds of shy, besides. Some people are introverted about themselves, but light up when they get onstage or in front of a camera. Lots of performers fall into that category. Kirk Cameron was almost too shy to get started, but once the camera was turned on, his shyness disappeared. New Kids on the Block's Jonathan Knight can be painfully shy in one-on-one situations, but once he gets up onstage and starts moving, there's no trace of it. In those cases, shyness is not a major obstacle.

Here's an idea to combat shyness. Change your focus to someone other than yourself. You'll find you're not quite so bashful. The next time you go to a party, don't worry about how you look or how others will judge you. Instead, go up to another person and make *her* feel comfortable. Ask questions, get to know someone else—understand that most people feel as awkward as you do. "Be a giving person," counsels Diane Hardin. "If you give of yourself to others, you put them at ease *and* come out of your shell at the same time." Agent Judy Savage agrees: "Decide you're going to make someone else have a great day—change the emphasis outward. That will go a long way toward solving the shyness problem!"

Another surefire cure for shyness is training. A good acting coach should bring out your true personality.

SO YOU WANT TO BE A STAR!

Knowing your craft gives you a sense of self-confidence. "Shyness will disappear if you've trained and you know your craft," advises Helen Garrett. "You can't change your basic personality, but shyness can be overcome—while you might get by being a wallflower at school, it'll never happen onstage."

More tips from the experts: "Get into plays, where personality plays a smaller role. Go to every audition for every single stage play. Get that experience. Sign up for speech classes, talk in front of people, get used to talking in front of adults."

YOUR TALENT

No question about it, talent plays a major role in whether or not you ever break into show biz. But what exactly *is* talent and how do you know if you've got enough to cut it? You may think you're a talented actor or actress, you may even be the toast of your small town, but how will the pros see you? While singing in the shower you may sound just like Paula Abdul, but would a record company agree in the cold, dry atmosphere of a recording studio?

Some people just know if they're talented, they have a sixth sense about it. They're born knowing it. Others aren't quite so sure. New Kids on the Block's Donnie Wahlberg feels, "Everyone has talent. Some people do things with theirs, others don't. But everyone has undeveloped talent from the day they're born." And, in fact, your teen years are a good time to test your talent. After all, you don't yet have the responsibility of having to earn a living!

If you think you've got the right stuff, but aren't sure it's enough, get feedback. Ask your school drama teacher to critique you, ask adults you respect for their honest opinions. Chances are, if you are truly talented, people will have told you already. But even if no one has said anything, don't feel you're out of it. If you've got the drive, the burning desire to continue, keep at it.

On the other hand, talent alone doesn't guarantee a star on the Hollywood Walk of Fame! You still need to work at it, to learn and develop it. More than anything, you must have determination, ambition, commitment, and burning desire. Add that to talent, a unique look, and an amiable personality—and you've got It!

FRED SAVAGE OF "THE WONDER YEARS" TELLS HOW IT HAPPENED!

"I never really wanted to get into the business, it was never a goal, it just happened. I was living in Glencoe, that's by Chicago, and when I was five years old, we heard about auditions being held at the local community center. My mom and I went down because we thought it would be a lot of fun.

"We had never done anything like that before, you know. It was for Oscar Meyer hot dogs and I remember eating a hot dog and then going for ice cream after that audition.

"We weren't, like competitive, in trying to get it, it was just for something to do. I didn't get the commercial. But it turned out that the director was a neighbor of ours, Bob Richter, and six months later he called me for a Pizza Hut commercial. I didn't get that either. And then, six months later, a year after the first one, he called me for a Pac-Man vitamins commercial. I was six and I got it.

"I signed up with the Emilia Lorence Agency when Bob mentioned to a casting director, Ken Carlson, that I had potential. Ken called up Linda Jack at that

FRED SAVAGE

agency. They signed me and I did commercials for about two years.

"When I was eight, I got my first movie, *The Boy Who Could Fly*. It was a lot of fun, I just really loved it. I went to Hollywood and met agents there and signed with the Iris Burton Agency. Then I did the movies *Vice Versa* and *The Princess Bride*. I was in the *Afterschool Special,* 'Runaway Ralph,' and a short-lived series called 'Morningstar, Eveningstar.'

"I like all kinds of acting, everything is pretty much similar, you know, movies of the week, TV series, movies. The real difference is between those and commercials. Even though I started making movies, I still was doing commercials and voiceovers and living at home with my family and going to school and playing sports, too. Next to acting, sports is my favorite thing to do. Name the sport and I can play it.

"I didn't really audition for 'The Wonder Years.' What happened was, the producers and director called Iris Burton up and gave her a script and said we'd like Fred to do this. So she read the script and she gave it to us and we all immediately fell in love with it. There's not that many great shows and this is one of them. We called Iris and we said we'd love to do it. So my dad and I went to California and we met with the producers and the directors and I rehearsed a few scenes with them. Then I went for network approval at ABC and I guess they liked me.

"At first, we stayed in an apartment in Los Angeles, just me and my mom. My dad, brother, and sister would come out periodically, on the weekends. They kind of commuted. But now we have a house in California, and my brother Ben and my sister Kala are both in the business, too. They're kind of up and coming. I have three aunts, uncles, and a bunch of cousins here. My grandparents are here, too. Only my dad can't be here all the time because he has an industrial real estate business in Chicago.

"There's not much time for hanging out because if I'm not on the set, I'm with a tutor, doing schoolwork. It's easier than in a regular classroom 'cause there's not a ton of kids. But it's harder on the tutor because he can't stand up and say one thing to the whole class. He has to come over to each of us—Jason, Josh, Danica, and me—and teach different things, because we're all on different levels.

"When I was in regular school in Glencoe, after I would come back from an acting assignment, the first day everyone would ask me a lot of questions. But then the next day things went back to normal and it's like I wasn't even gone. I like that because I don't want them to treat me any better or worse because I'm on television.

"To me, acting's just like a hobby, kinda, and it's just something I do. I miss my regular school sometimes, but I get to go places. I'm just a normal kid doing something he likes to do."

CHAPTER 3

IN TRAINING

Getting ready for a career in show biz is just like preparing for a career in any field—to get in the game, you need to be trained! There are very few people born with such astounding natural talent that they don't need any kind of training. Of the stars you know, even a Tom Cruise or a River Phoenix—two of the most highly regarded "natural" performers—have had some instruction. Another young natural, Winona Ryder, was actually discovered at drama class at the American Conservatory Theater in San Francisco doing a monologue as a class exercise.

Talent not only needs to be shaped and developed but also needs to be exercised. You've got to act to learn to act; you've got to sing or dance or do stand-up comedy to learn to do it better. And you must keep practicing to keep from getting rusty!

Would it surprise you to know that many of today's top stars, even those who are on TV series or in the movies, still go for acting lessons when they can? Singers continue with voice lessons, musicians, too. You never stop learning.

Here's where you start.

AT SCHOOL AND IN PRIVATE LESSONS

School plays as well as the school chorus, band, or church or temple choir are obvious places, for nearly every school and house of worship in every small town has some kind of performing group.

Try out at every single opportunity. If you're an aspiring singer or musician, perhaps the school play includes music—ask if you can be the accompanist. Debbie Gibson used to play piano for her school's performances. She volunteered to do it; she didn't wait for someone to ask her! Paula Abdul started doing choreography for the plays in her elementary school.

If you don't get a part, see if you can be part of the backstage crew. Help out with the scenery, work the lights or the sound system, or even draw the curtain— do anything that puts you near the action. If you love performing, you'll love anything connected with it.

The next step is drama school or private acting, voice, or music lessons. You may have heard the reasoning that acting lessons ruin "naturalness," but most professionals don't agree with that rationale. They feel that, especially after young performers outgrow their "cute" stage, all actors need some guidance. And certainly every singer can benefit from coaching.

The main purpose of acting classes is to help you feel confident about yourself in front of other people. They should give you the ability to be vulnerable and uninhibited in front of an audience and, as Kevin McDermott puts it, "teach you to show real emotion in unreal situations."

SO YOU WANT TO BE A STAR!

Actor Robert Rusler (of the TV show "The Outsiders") said his acting classes "gave me the self-confidence to go out on a limb and take a chance, to break my emotional barriers."

Agent Vicki Light adds, "Acting classes should also teach you something called *technique,* which saves your life as an actor. It gets you through the rough spots, like when you're supposed to feel real emotional about something but you don't feel anything, you rely on technique."

It would be a big mistake, however, to jump into just any acting class. There are many wonderful schools around the country with superb teachers, but there are just as many rip-off joints whose sole purpose is to separate you from your money! And there are others with good intentions that may not be right for you. It's your job to investigate. Here's what you should look for.

A CHECKLIST FOR CLASSES

Basically, acting classes should have a core curriculum of improvisation, scene study, theater games, and, perhaps, cold reading skills. Improvisational classes do just that—you improvise. In scene study classes you learn how to interpret the lines on a page and make each line look spontaneous. No one should tell you how to read a line—that comes from yourself.

The classes you sign up for should be with other kids about the same age as you. Kevin McDermott divides his classes like this: 9–12 year olds, 13–15, and 16–19. The scripts you work from, he warns, should be "age appropriate." In other words, you should be able to relate to the stuff you're saying.

Class size is important. Classes that have more than twelve to fifteen students are just too large. You won't have enough opportunities to perform.

The school you enroll in should also have specific classes that teach interview techniques so you'll know what to expect at an audition. Some schools give courses in the differences between acting for commercials and acting for TV and movies. That can be very helpful. Another helpful course is dialect training. If you have a regional accent it's going to hurt you. Classes that rid you of your natural accent are a plus.

Some schools use cameras and videotape recorders in class, and while that is important, don't be dazzled. "Good acting classes," warns Kevin McDermott, "are not necessarily the ones that look the best with all sorts of high-tech equipment. I do almost no camera work with my students because they tend to get too critical and self-conscious. They think too much and react too little! Instead, look for classes where the teachers interact well with the students."

If you're an aspiring rock 'n' roller, you may need a voice teacher and a voice coach and a teacher for your instrument. More about that in Chapter 9.

FINDING THE RIGHT PLACES

So how do you find these wonderful schools and coaches that offer exactly what you should be looking for?

• Ask around. Talk to friends who are taking classes—see if they're happy and why. Contact a nearby university and ask the head of the drama or music department to recommend schools in the area. Call local theater groups for some feedback.

- Research. There may be franchised theatrical agents in your area. In the next chapter you will learn how to find these agents. Contact a few and ask, "Who's qualified to teach acting or voice in my area?"

Looking in the phone directory might seem like another resource, but most pros will tell you that's not the way to go. Advertising costs money—and that cost will be directly passed on to you.

Speaking of cost, private schools and coaches are an expense—but they should not be in excess of about twenty-five dollars a class. The best classes in Hollywood aren't much more than that. Comparison shop! Same goes for voice or instrumental lessons. Prices vary, so look around and compare.

- Check them out! When you find a school or coach that you think fits your requirements, do four more things before you sign on. Check with the Better Business Bureau to make sure no one's lodged any complaints against the school or any teachers. Ask to talk with people who go there or people who used to go there. Find out what their refund policy is and, most importantly, ask to audit or sit in on a class before you join. Good, reputable schools will allow you to do that. Auditing a class may cost a bit, but can save a whole bunch in the long run.

DON'T GET TAKEN: CLASSIC RIP-OFFS

There are disreputable schools, and here are some warning signals. Avoid acting schools or classes that make you any guarantees. No one in show biz can guarantee you anything. A guarantee is a sign of a rip-off. Beware of any school that comes with a "package deal." The package may include a photographer for the photos you'll need. The school should not be affiliated with any one photographer.

Also, classes that teach poise, charm, and how to dress have nothing to do with acting. They will *not* give you the necessary skills for a career in show biz!

There are schools that ask for a lot of money to print your photo in a book they *say* agents and casting directors will see. All the pros say that is *not* the way they discover new talent. For the most part they never look through those books at all. Also there are "services" that for a fee will put your photo on local cable TV, which they say casting directors will see. Nonsense! Casting directors work during the day and don't sit around watching cable TV. There is no shortcut to show biz, but there are lots of ways to get ripped off. These are a few of them.

PAYING FOR LESSONS

Okay, you've found a good place, but there's still a major problem. Even though the price of classes seems fair, you can't afford them. This doesn't mean you have to give up. Many good schools give scholarships to talented individuals. Be honest, tell them you'd like to sign up but can't afford it. Ask if they'd let you audition for a scholarship? You could also offer to work in exchange for lessons—do some clerical office work such as Xeroxing or filing. It doesn't hurt to ask.

Of course, you can try to earn the money yourself to pay for lessons. A weekend baby-sitting job could net you enough, or a paper route, perhaps. If your grand-parents or relatives usually give you a gift for your birthday or holidays, ask if they would give you money for acting lessons instead. Be creative—if there's a will, there's a way and you'll find it. Natural-ly, tell your parents about your plans.

BETTER NONE THAN THE WRONG KIND

It's entirely possible that after searching you won't find an acting school or music coach who'll properly prepare you for a career in show biz. In that case, forget about formal lessons—for a while at least. It's better not to have lessons than to have the wrong kind, or even worse, to get cheated.

This doesn't mean you have to stop following your dream. You can always learn by doing: try out for plays in school, in the parks and recreation depart-ments around town, and in community centers. In Chapter 5 we'll talk about community and regional theater and summer stock, all of which you might want to look into.

OTHER KINDS OF TRAINING

Part of your training for a show-biz career involves lessons other than straight acting, voice, or instru-mental. Any kind of lessons are helpful, for the more skills you have, the more chances you have at breaking in. Take speech class in school because any time you get up and speak to a group of people is good practice. Joining the debate team is a good idea, too. Dance lessons are especially helpful as are gymnastics, swimming, even skiing and karate. Aerobics help you shape up and are great for building stamina. Debbie Gibson's voice teacher has her working with weights; Tiffany and Paula Abdul work out all the time.

Sports of any kind are worthwhile. Aside from mastering the skill, you learn how to work as part of a team. Any performing you will do is teamwork too.

Anything you do for fun or profit can come in handy. You might land a commercial because you're a great skateboarder or know how to juggle, ride a bike, or bowl. One agent got a call for an actor who could toss a pizza pie in the air. She contacted her clients who'd worked in fast-food places. The actor who'd made pizzas got the gig.

The most important experience you can get is an education! Not just because your folks are on your case about it, but because it's vital for any actor or singer to be educated.

You need to be well-rounded in order to portray a variety of characters. You need to "know a little about a lot," says Vicki Light, "and draw on your experiences and knowledge."

A good vocabulary is crucial to understanding the words in the script. Because his formal education was lacking, Tom Cruise often carries a dictionary with him when he's studying a new script.

Also, you must think beyond acting when you're in your teens. Someday you'll be an adult and expected to know about events in history and in science. You'll need to know how to write intelligently. You'll even need math skills. Don't neglect your education; you're only shortchanging yourself as a performer.

SO YOU WANT TO BE A STAR!

AT-HOME TRAINING

Are there things you can do at home to get in training for a show-biz career? You bet there are—and they're all fun to do as well. Putting on plays with your friends is a great idea. Get together with a bunch of kids once a week for play readings—take out books of plays from the library and act them out for family, neighbors, and friends, or for your church or synagogue. You might even find you enjoy directing other kids in plays.

Do you have access to a video recorder? Make a mini-movie out of your play. That's exactly what such superstars as Charlie Sheen, Emilio Estevez, and Sean Penn used to do as young teenagers. They'd write their own scripts, round up buddies to be the actors, and video them. It was good training and good fun!

Aspiring rockers have traditionally formed amateur groups with like-minded buddies.

There are exercises you can do all by yourself to help get ready. Read as much good literature as you can. Read dramatic and comic monologues out loud. Get used to the sound of your own voice, express yourself in other people's words—read novels out loud, even comic books and cereal boxes! Have fun with voices, try out different accents. One word of caution: Don't perform in front of a mirror. That tends to make you pose, which is not the same as acting. Actors need an audience, so read to anyone who'll listen!

Go to movies, see plays, go to concerts, and dance recitals, too. Try to decide what you liked about a particular piece, what made it special for you. Watch good (as in well-acted and well-written) TV shows like "The Wonder Years," "L.A. Law," "thirtysomething" and "Life Goes On."

Observe humanity! Try to figure out what makes people tick, why they do and say the things they do. Start with your own family. Then store your observations in "the toolboxes of your mind" for future reference when you're called on to bring life to different characters.

HOW POP STAR PAULA ABDUL CHOREOGRAPHED AN AMAZING CAREER!

Dance was Paula Abdul's very first love. As a tiny tot, her favorite movie was Gene Kelly's *Singing in the Rain*. She tried to mimic the dance routines.

When she was six years old she passed a dance studio on her way to school and got her mom, a former concert pianist, to sign her and older sister Wendy up for lessons.

For Paula, those lessons—which included ballet, tap, jazz, and modern—"were like a reward to me, a special treat." She showed enormous natural ability very early. She even caught on to her sister's more complicated routines after seeing them just once.

In elementary school the native Los Angeleno got involved in all the school productions, acting, singing, and dancing. When word of her special dance talent got out to teachers, she was asked to choreograph routines. By sixth grade, she'd staged an entire musical.

While continuing with her dance lessons, Paula added acting and singing lessons. She was in commu-

PAULA ABDUL

nity theater and spent many summers touring the country with a group of budding performers called The Young Americans.

"Ever since I was a kid," she explains, "I've always wanted to do it all. I've always had the fire in me. I wanted to be onstage, singing, dancing, acting. And I I knew I would get my chance." It's doubtful that she knew her chance would come through cheerleading!

At Van Nuys High School, things weren't always easy. Because of her exotic looks, she was often caught in the middle between ethnic groups. But popular Paula was voted class president one year, student council member, and head cheerleader. She used her dance background to create new steps for the cheerleading squad and devised routines that even the least agile cheerleader could master.

By the time she started college at Cal State Northridge, Paula's goal was to be in show biz and sportscasting. A self-admitted "total sports nut," Paula found a way to combine her twin passions. She auditioned for the Los Angeles Lakers cheerleading squad, the Laker Girls. Not only did Paula beat out hundreds of contenders for a spot on the squad, but by midseason, she was choreographing their routines. Paula turned the Laker Girls into a dance team.

Many Lakers season ticketholders were entertainment industry pros, and Paula Abdul was getting the kind of exposure she couldn't pay for.

But it would be four years until she got her first big break. The Jacksons (Michael's brothers) were preparing a video for their song "Torture." They, too, were Lakers ticketholders and were very impressed with the cheerleaders' dazzling moves. They asked her to choreograph their video.

"I was floored," she remembers. "I'd never done anything like a video." It was intimidating, too, teaching Jackie, Jermaine, Tito, Marlon, and Randy to dance the Abdul way, but she did.

It's assumed that Paula got her next big break, with Janet Jackson, through the brothers, but that's not what happened. In fact, it was a full year later that an executive at Janet's record company also saw Paula—yes, at a Lakers game—and asked her to work with the youngest Jackson.

Paula was thrilled and worked with Janet choreographing videos for her *Control* album. Even though the two young women became personal friends, Janet didn't open any pop-music doors for Paula.

She continued with the Lakers. All in all, she put in six years with the team. What was that about an overnight success? During this time Paula started recording demos and shopping them around to record companies. In one year's time they were all rejected.

She also continued to work as a choreographer. She staged dance scenes in several movies, including Eddie Murphy's *Coming to America,* worked with Steve Winwood, Duran Duran, Kool and the Gang, ZZ Top, and George Michael. The more she worked with singers, the more she wanted to *be* one.

The executives who'd approached her about Janet Jackson decided to form their own record company, and one of the first acts they signed was Paula Abdul. As Paula first got into recording, she still had many dance commitments. For a while she was juggling four or five assignments at once, including choreographing "The Tracey Ullman Show," for which she won an Emmy Award.

But hard work and balancing projects is part of

what makes Paula run—she admittedly thrives on it. Her debut LP, *Forever Your Girl,* a slow starter at first, has sold over two million copies and spawned several smash singles and a remixed dance LP. She's been signed as a spokesperson for L.A. Gear and has received more awards (including four MTV Awards) than she has room for on her mantel.

But Paula's had her share of disappointments, even now that she's a big star. The very plum assignment of her life—choreographing the movie version of the play *Evita,* which was to star Meryl Streep—was plucked away when Meryl bowed out. The project's now on hold indefinitely.

She has new goals, including directing and starring in a Broadway musical and in feature films.

Paula's words of wisdom to would-be stars: "If you really believe in yourself and work hard, somehow, some way, things will happen for you."

CHAPTER 4

ALL ABOUT AGENTS
AND MANAGERS

You hear about agents and managers because stars talk about them in interviews and thank them profusely on awards shows. It seems as if an agent's what you really need to get started in this business. Find an agent, and presto you're in.

Not exactly. It is true that you'll need representation at some point, but a good theatrical or booking agent or a reputable manager can be hard to find. Once you find one, it's even harder to get that person to take you on as a client. And even if he or she does, there's no guarantee you'll be happy or that you'll get any jobs! Did anyone say this was going to be easy?

The terms *agent* and *manager* are tossed around freely, but most beginners don't have a very clear idea of what the difference between them is, how you actually find and hook up with them, and what they can and can't do for you. You're about to find out.

But first things first:

Neither an agent nor a manager can "get" you a job. *You* get you a job. An agent's job is to know about upcoming projects, get you an audition for a job, and negotiate the terms of your employment. A manager's job is to shape and guide your career as a whole. Managers need good contacts with agents, and agents need good contacts with casting directors. Now, to the nitty-gritty.

ALL ABOUT AGENTS

A theatrical agent is someone with many clients who receives breakdowns from casting directors describing the type of actors needed to fill specific roles in TV shows, movies, commercials, videos, and stage productions. A good agent will be well connected with lots of casting directors. The agent will then pick several actors from his client list who seem to fit the role requirements and send their photos to the casting director in hopes of securing auditions for his or her clients.

Should one of the clients land a job, the agent will then negotiate the fee and set the terms of employment. Smart agents use good judgment about which clients to send on which interviews. They also know how to make good deals, and they have excellent personal relationships with key industry people—not only casting directors, but producers, directors, script writers, and, of course, reputable managers. They're on top of what's going on in the industry, which movies are going to be made before the casting process begins. They often "campaign" for their clients to land hot roles. After they've sent clients on auditions, they call the casting director to get feedback.

A good agent can be from a small agency or a large one—the best agent is one who believes in you.

The only kind of agent you want is someone who is franchised by the performers' unions and licensed by the state. That's a key way of knowing an agent is reputable. To become franchised, agents must follow some pretty heavy-duty rules and regulations. They must be bonded and fingerprinted. They may be listed in the phone book, but they may *not* advertise to solicit clients, teach acting classes, or do any acting or producing in their home state. The only kind of contract a reputable agent is allowed to sign with you is the standard SAG or AFTRA contract. It provides for a one-year agreement between you and the agent with a three-year option to continue. It includes a clause whereby if the agent has not procured any work for you in ninety days, you may leave the agency. It also limits their fee to ten percent of your earnings—if they've gotten you the job. In other words, only after you get paid, do they get paid.

NEVER, EVER, PAY AN AGENT UPFRONT MONEY FOR ANYTHING.

You don't pay someone to become your agent. Ever.

An agent who asks for any money from you *before* you've worked is not legitimate. "Run fast and run far" is the advice given by all reputable agents, if you find yourself in that situation.

ALL ABOUT MANAGERS

Managers, on the other hand, are not licensed or franchised in any way. There are no rules governing what they can and can't do, or how much they can commission. Many people call themselves managers —you'll even hear of a celebrity's parent being his or her manager.

SO YOU WANT TO BE A STAR!

A manager acts as a "middle man" between you and, hopefully, several agents. Managers generally have fewer clients to represent than agents do and often spend more time with each individual. The best managers prepare you for meetings with agents and casting directors. They guide you in terms of how to look, how to dress, how to get ready for an audition. Many go over scripts with you, teach you to work with video cameras, help choose which photos you're going to use, teach you the basics of professionalism.

Diane Hardin is one of Hollywood's best regarded managers. She only half jokingly describes her relationship with her clients: "I'm their psychiatrist, wardrobe person, coach, and career consultant." Likewise, Jerry Silverhardt, who discovered Tom Cruise and now works with Richard Grieco, says, "I groom my clients. I decide what they can handle. Whenever they're not ready for something, I coach them."

Good managers have good relationships with agents. Although they can't negotiate fees themselves, they can and do work with agents who do negotiate. Jerry Silverhardt says he helped structure Richard Grieco's first deal with "21 Jump Street." "Richard was originally only hired for six episodes. I made sure that just in case they decided to extend his contract, that his pay scale went up." Good thing—as everyone knows, Fox TV kept Richard on for the whole season and then gave him his own show, "Booker." Now he's making movies!

Good managers are also similarly well connected with casting directors and inside starmakers.

Although there are no official rules governing what a manager's commission should be, there are some "rules of thumb" *generally accepted throughout the industry.* Most managers charge between fifteen and twenty percent of what you make. A few charge twenty-five percent. Music managers have been known to get more.

You strike your own deal. However, as with an agent, *never pay a manager for anything, unless, while under his or her tutelage you've gotten a paying job.* You don't pay anyone to become your manager. Ever.

Although there are no specific managerial contracts, many good managers take their clients on for a three-year period, with a three-year option to renew after that. The best, most reputable managers don't even ask you to sign anything until they've helped you hook up with an agent *and* you've gotten some work. Of course, those who do that put themselves in a precarious position—what's to stop a client from benefiting from their expertise and then refusing to sign with them? Many managers put their trust in you, just as you put your trust in them.

DO YOU REALLY NEED THEM?

Do you really need an agent, a manager, or both? In order to work in any network TV show, movie, or national commercial, you absolutely need an agent. No question about it. Nearly all productions fall under SAG or AFTRA (American Federation of Radio and TV Artists) jurisdiction and they simply won't hire you if you're not represented by a legitimate agent.

But it is *not* necessary, or perhaps even advisable, to go after an agent when you're first starting out. It makes more sense to look for work where you don't need an agent—community and regional theater, dinner theater, summer stock, college productions, plus locally made or cable commercials. First, if you don't live in a big city, chances are there *are* no franchised agents around. Second, most agents won't take you on as a client unless you've got some stage experience under your belt!

What about a manager? Well, there are those who swear by them, who say they wouldn't have gotten anywhere without the nurturing of their personal manager. Stars like Chad Allen, Corey Haim, Chris Young, Matt Dillon, Patrick Swayze, Ralph Macchio, New Kids on the Block, Debbie Gibson, and Tiffany all have, or have had, managers. Some have remained in happy, equitable situations with their managers; others have had major falling-outs. Some stars who didn't go with professional managers are Johnny Depp, Alyssa Milano, River Phoenix, Fred Savage, and Michael J. Fox.

A manager can be helpful if you don't know anything about the business or if your parents aren't available to protect and oversee your career. A manager should take the time to advise and prepare you for the world of show biz—agents usually don't have that kind of time. Yet there are exceptions—there are some agents who will guide and nurture your career. If you're lucky enough to have one of those, you don't need a manager, too.

THE GREAT AGENT/MANAGER HUNT

Finding an agent or manager requires lots of work. Getting one to represent you takes even more! You're ahead of the game if you have any contacts at all in the entertainment industry. If you know people connected with show biz who know agents, ask for their help first. Nearly every agent or manager will see someone who's recommended by a contact.

If you have no contacts, however, your first step should be to write to SAG in Hollywood (the address is in Chapter 14). For a nominal fee, they can send you a list of franchised agents all over the U.S.A. or tell you where the nearest branch office is to get a list of agents. (If you live in Canada there's a similar union called ACTRA and they can be helpful in the same way.) Send a letter along with a self-addressed stamped envelope, plus one dollar, asking for a list of agents in your area who represent teens and adults. There are agents in seventeen states (including Hawaii)—all are located in big cities. There are hundreds in California and New York. Get the list, and if you live within an hour's drive of a franchised agent, send a photo and résumé.

Call local TV stations, newspapers, and ad agencies, asking which talent agencies they use for local ads.

Word of mouth is another way to find agents and managers. Ask everyone you know—your drama or dance teacher, or your voice coach. Call the nearest university with a drama department and ask for suggestions—call your local community theater group.

Whenever you do get a suggestion for an agent, call SAG and see if the person is franchised.

Finding a reputable manager is trickier because you don't have SAG to help you. You must be extra careful. Go by recommendations of people you respect and trust. Ask agents for their suggestions on managers—check with the Better Business Bureau.

SO YOU WANT TO BE A STAR!

There is an organization called the National Conference of Personal Managers. You may want to get in touch with either their East or West Coast branch for a suggestion, or you may want to check on the reputation of someone you're considering. Write: **Joe Rapp, National Conference of Personal Managers, 1650 Broadway, New York, NY 10019,** or **Tami Lynn, Conference of Personal Managers, 4527 Park Allegra, Calabasas Park, CA 91302.**

Go with a parent to meet a potential manager. Have a list of specific questions. Find out how the manager is prepared to help you. Ask which agents they work with and call those agents. Ask who else they represent and get references. Jerry Silverhardt urges potential clients to even call casting directors and inquire about his reputation.

Don't be dazzled by a fast-talking salesman who promises you the moon. No one in show biz should be making any promises. It can't be repeated too often that you *never pay anyone to manage you.* They earn a commission only if you work. And never sign any managerial contract without a good entertainment lawyer.

HOW TO CONTACT AGENTS AND MANAGERS: PHOTOS AND RÉSUMÉS

There is an accepted way to solicit agents and reputable managers. You send them a photograph of yourself, plus a copy of your résumé, and a cover letter. Put a sturdy piece of cardboard in the envelope so your photo doesn't get bent. It looks more professional, too!

Your photograph may be either in black and white or in color. It can be a snapshot taken by your mom or even a school photo, as long as it's clear, well lit, and really looks like you. Hold it up to the mirror. Be honest. The picture shouldn't be too posed and it should give some indication of your personality. You should not wear a bathing suit, sunglasses, or hat. You shouldn't be wearing a lot of makeup. You should be as natural-looking and wholesome as possible.

If your photo is smaller than an eight-by-ten, glue it onto a larger sheet of paper or cardboard and write your name on it.

You don't need to spend a lot of money on professional photos when you're trying to get an agent. Every reputable agent will tell you that a snapshot is just fine when you're starting. Once the agent has taken you on as a client, you'll need professional photos. Each agent has his own idea of what a professional photo should look like, so having your photos done ahead of time is a waste of money. All agents and managers should give you a list of several photographers to choose from.

Your résumé (pronounced res-oo-may) is a typed (or neatly handwritten) list of any and all acting experience you've had. It must be glued, stapled, or taped to the back of your photo. Put down school plays, community theater, church or synagogue productions, neighborhood plays, talent shows, recitals— any and all performing you've done. Always include the name of the theater (or school, etc.) you worked in and the part you played.

In addition, list any training you've had—who you studied with, where, and when and what courses you took.

SO YOU WANT TO BE A STAR!

Put down any and all skills you have, from bike-riding to skateboarding. Don't exaggerate your skills, however. Don't say you can roller-skate if you've only been around the rink once.

Your résumé must also include your hair and eye color, height, weight, and, of course, your name. *Don't* put a home address on it because you never know whose hands it may fall into. *Don't* put a home phone number on it for the same reason. *Do* put a service number down or the work number of your mom or dad.

Here's a sample of what a beginner's résumé might look like.

MINDY PAIGE

(605) 763–9114 (Mrs. Paige's work number)

Height: 5′ 2″   Hair: Strawberry blond
Weight: 100 lbs.   Eyes: Blue

Theater

Bye Bye Birdie	Supporting Role	Syosset Theater, 1988
Romeo and Juliet	Juliet	Peoria H.S., 1989
Annie	Orphan Julie	YMHA of Peoria, 1990

Training

Young Actor's Space	Drama	(Presently)
The Dance Studio	Jazz, Ballet	(Presently)
Voices R Us	Musical Theater	(1987–1989)

Skills

Tennis, horseback riding, Ping-Pong, roller skating, bowling, soccer, double-dutch jump rope, Frisbee tossing, piano.

Your cover letter is included to set you apart from the hundreds of other hopefuls soliciting agents and managers each day! Keep it short and well-written, but do let your personality come through. Tell them how you heard of them, why you want to be in show biz and why you think they should meet you.

Don't hesitate to be creative with your cover letter. Send a funny greeting card instead of a letter; if you're artistic, decorate it. One aspirant even sent a newsletter about herself! Anything you can do to make yourself stand out is a plus.

You can also send a *videotape* of your work, but don't send your only copy. Odds are, you won't get it back.

Reality check time. Agents and managers receive an average of fifty photos every single day. They eventually go through all of them, but they only call the ones they're interested in interviewing. Otherwise, you probably will not hear from them. But here's a great tip.

Include a self-addressed, stamped *postcard* in your packet. On it write:

Thanks for considering me. I understand you're busy, but please take the time to check one of the following:

_____You are interested and will call, or

_____You are interested and want me to call you.

Unfortunately, you aren't interested because:

_____Not unique-looking enough;

_____Not enough theatrical credits/training;

_____Conflicts with others in your agency.

SO YOU WANT TO BE A STAR!

(The last choice means they have enough blue-eyed strawberry blondes already signed up. Agents and managers look for a variety of types to represent.) If you send that postcard and don't get a call from a prospective agent, at least you may know why.

There is another good way to solicit representation. Many agents and managers attend local plays, recitals, and drama workshop presentations. Ralph Macchio's original manager spotted him at a dance recital and Monique Lanier got the role of Paige in "Life Goes On" because a casting director saw her in a college play. So it happens. But you don't need to sit back and hope influential people come to see you perform—you can invite them. Make up fliers and mail them to agents and managers telling about an upcoming performance. Be sure to include a photo of yourself and tell them which part you'll be playing.

You can also submit your photo and résumé to local independent casting directors and ad agencies.

Take any initiative you can. There are no guarantees, but you increase your odds by trying.

AN INTERVIEW WITH AN AGENT

Let's say you've done everything you're supposed to and you've gotten the call—an agent wants to set up an appointment to interview you. Here's what to expect.

The interview will probably take place in the agent's office. Be sure to have a parent or some other adult with you for your own protection. Be on time. Dress casually—no party dresses or wild punky outfits. Go easy on the makeup and jewelry. Bring a monologue

57

or scene from a script you've practiced—you may or may not be asked to read. Best to be prepared.

Expect to have to wait to be seen. One agent purposely makes aspiring actors wait for an hour. She's not being cruel. "It's a test," she explains, "to see how they'll do in an audition situation. When they go up for a role with a casting director, they'd better be prepared to wait!" You should also be prepared for interruptions, lots of them! Agents are busy, phones ring all the time—don't take it personally.

Eventually, you'll be called in to meet the agent. Your parent can't come with you. Most agents realize you're nervous and will try to ease the tension by chatting with you. You might be asked to "cold read" something you've never seen before, or you might be asked if you've prepared anything to read.

What are they looking for? Since the agent called you, something about you has struck a chord—he or she wants to know more. "I go by personality and attitude," says Natalie Rosson, "but most important-ly, acting ability." Agent Booh Schut concurs. "Talent is number one. I will represent teenagers with tremen-dous ability." Agent Carollyn DeVore clocks in with "I'll sign them up if there's something about them, an edge, a personality, a look." When little bundle of energy Tempestt Bledsoe of "The Cosby Show" first walked into an agent's office, she was so spirited and animated that she "took the place over." The agent signed her up on the spot.

After your interview an agent might want to meet your parent. That's usually a good sign—it means he's still interested. If he does want to sign you up, check first with SAG to make sure the agent is in good standing with them. Ask if the agency sends clients for commercials and voiceover work as well as TV and movie jobs. If you want to do commercials, you may be disappointed to sign with an agent and find out that she doesn't do commercials! Ask for a list of other clients represented and contact a few of them. You want to know if they're satisfied, if they're being sent out on auditions, if they're working. You want an agent with a good track record!

Decide how *you* feel about this person. You have to like the person who'll be representing you. When it comes time to sign a contract, have your parent be sure it's a standard SAG contract (it will say on it).

If you leave the interview and don't hear anything, you might want to call and find out why. If the agent has decided not to take you on at this time, don't give up. Try other agencies, try again next year!

WHAT IF YOU CAN'T GET
AN AGENT OR MANAGER

What if you can't find anyone to represent you? Does that mean you're finished? Not at all. Though it may be hard to believe, you may actually be lucky. For your route to show-biz stardom is going to have to be through theater. It may take you longer, but here's a little secret. Odds are, with all the experience and training you'll pick up along the way, you'll have a longer and more successful career.

TIP-OFFS TO RIP-OFFS:
HERE'S WHAT TO AVOID

- A manager (or agent) who insists you take acting lessons with him or her, insists you use one particular photographer, or asks you for money upfront.
- Agents and managers who advertise. Agents aren't allowed to, good managers almost never do.
- Referral services. You may receive something in the mail, or see an ad in a newspaper for a service that gets you photos and sends them to agents and managers. For that, they charge a fee. Forget it! You can do all that yourself.
- Private situations. If a potential manager invites you to his house and tells you to come alone, run the other way! Never do anything you feel uncomfortable doing. Trust your instincts and don't be fooled. There *are* people out there who will take advantage of you.
- Signing anything (other than a standard SAG contract) before it's been scrutinized by a lawyer. If you're under eighteen, it's illegal for you to sign a contract anyway. Also, don't bind yourself to any one person for a long period of time; you never know what may happen in the future.

HOW SOME STARS FOUND—OR DIDN'T FIND—
THEIR AGENTS AND MANAGERS

C. Thomas Howell (Soul Man) has a dad who is a Hollywood stunt man. He brought young Tommy in to see an agent, who turned him down because he was "tall for his age and had no experience!" Tommy was told to get some theatrical experience under his belt and try again. He did, and eventually signed with another agent.

Johnny Depp ("21 Jump Street") came to Hollywood to be a rock singer. He had no agent until he became friends with actor Nicolas Cage. Nick introduced Johnny to *his* agent who signed him up immediately!

Neil Patrick Harris ("Doogie Howser, M.D.") came to his agent's attention through the recommendation of a script writer she knew.

Kirk and Candace Cameron ("Growing Pains" and "Full House") met their agent through one of her clients who was a Cameron neighbor.

Lecy Goranson ("Roseanne") was taking an after-school class at Chicago's Piven Workshop. One of her teachers invited an agent to come see her. She did and Lecy was on her way.

NEIL PATRICK HARRIS
How "Doogie" Did It!

"I grew up in the small town of Ruidoso, New Mexico. When I was, like, five or six, my parents took me into Albuquerque to see a traveling production of the show *Annie*. And something just clicked in my mind when I saw it. I made my parents get me the original cast album and the movie album and the book about it, everything about *Annie*. From then on I got interested in acting.

"It didn't surprise my parents because I was always one to entertain. I'm a juggler and a magician. I'm always trying to get attention! My mom and dad are both real interested in acting, too. They're not actors, they're lawyers, but they do community theater in New Mexico.

"When I was about in the third grade, my brother's junior high school was putting on *The Wizard Of Oz*, and my mom was taking him and a couple of his friends to try out for the Munchkins. I was just hanging around and they needed someone to play the dog, Toto, so they got me to do that. I wore kneepads

NEIL PATRICK HARRIS

and a dog suit. But I was in it most of the time and I got to bark. That was my first acting job!

"After that I was in all the plays at my school and I started performing in the one little community theater near where we lived. I even got to assistant-direct a play, which was a lot of fun and hard work. Kind of aggravating at times, but it was really satisfying.

"My drama teacher at school suggested that during the summer I go to a high school drama camp in Las Cruces that New Mexico State University was sponsoring called the American Southwest Theatre Company Drama Camp. By the time we called, it was starting the next week and I was the second-to-last person to sign up. I took improv classes and practiced audition pieces and took acting and movement classes. It was a week-long thing and you don't ever really sleep and you learn so much, it's great.

"A screenwriter named Mark Medoff was in residence at the camp the week I was there and it just so happened he was writing a movie called *Clara's Heart* at the time. There was a part for a teenage boy, and Mark thought I might fit it. So Mark talked to my parents and said that he wanted me to read for it. So we got a videotape of me doing some scenes with Mark and they sent it up to Los Angeles.

"Everything happened very quickly in one way— but took a long time in another way. Mark sent the tape to the producer of the movie in L.A. who was good friends with an agent named Booh Schut. We went up to meet her and she liked me and we liked her so I signed on with her agency. This all happened when I was fourteen.

"Anyway, it took a long time between the time Mark first tested me and I got the role in *Clara's*

Heart. My agent told me that some people at the movie studio didn't want me for the role and tested hundreds of other kids. But then there were some personnel changes at the studio and I ended up getting the part and working with Whoopi Goldberg. But in between signing with Booh and starting *Clara's Heart,* I was on the TV show 'Throb'—that was my first professional job—and then I was in some TV movies.

"I'm amazed that this all happened. I've been very lucky. All the time I was doing this stuff we were still able to live in New Mexico, and that's why, originally, we said we'd never take a TV series if it was offered. Everyone said, 'Don't do a series 'cause you'll move out to L.A. and then this will happen and that will happen and it will all be downhill from there.' But we just couldn't pass up 'Doogie Howser, M.D.' It's a really classy piece and we've always admired (the creator) Steven Bochco. Plus I felt the character of Doogie has a lot of possibilities and ways to go. He's a normal kid in extraordinary circumstances. And in at least one way he's like me. He ends up being around a lot of adults and I think a lot of kids that work in this business spend more of their time with adults than with kids their own age. Unless they're fortunate to be on a show with a lot of kids, which I'm not.

"I'm told they tested hundreds of kids for 'Doogie' and they weren't sure who to go with, but I'm glad I got it. The cast gets along great. Of course it did happen that we had to move to Los Angeles, at least while the show is being filmed. But my mom and dad took leaves of absence from their jobs and came with me; my brother's in college in New Mexico, so he stayed there. I'm lucky that my parents are very supportive. We want to make sure that our family stays together, 'cause that would be the worst, if they stayed in New Mexico and I went to California. It would tear the family apart. We want to make sure that our family and schoolwork come before this.

"I miss being in a classroom with other kids, I miss my friends in New Mexico, my real true friends that are great. We have a lot of fun, we do a lot of stuff together, drive around, 'cause in New Mexico you can get your license at fifteen. We rent movies, go watch dollar movies, play cards, do normal things.

"If there's a downside to this business I would say that that's it for me, having to be away from my friends and family. As for auditions, I learned not to take them so seriously. You can get all wrapped up in them, which can be kind of bad. If you try out for a part and you don't get it, you can't bang your head against a wall. You have to go on and do something else. Besides, being a kid actor, this really isn't my profession yet, it's just a hobby. I'm going to school and doing this on the side. It's gotten to be a big 'side,' but I can't take it that seriously.

"I hope I don't get typecast as 'Doogie Howser' forever because, someday, I want to go to New York and star in a Broadway musical. Try my luck in the Big Apple. That's my dream."

CHAPTER 5

THE PLAY'S THE THING!

Whether or not your goal is to get an agent or manager right away, there's not a pro in the business who doesn't recommend doing theater.

Doing plays is a great way to see if you really like performing, if a show-biz life is for you. Though it may be your dream, there's no real way of knowing if you should pursue it until you actually have some experience.

For the most part, you don't need any sort of representation to do theater—no agents or managers need be involved, which is certainly a relief if you live in a place where there aren't any. How you look is not a major factor—neither is your personality. This is the area of show biz where looks and personality count least.

Theater teaches you performance skills and discipline, which may make all the difference when your "big break" comes along. Says Warner Brothers casting director DeeDee Bradley, "There's no substitute for theatrical training. All the thousands of kids that come to Hollywood and don't make it are the ones who are not prepared, who are not trained." Indeed, big-time Hollywood casting people feel a lot more comfortable choosing someone with theater experience than without it.

So do agents. When agents look through the hundreds of photos and resumes that cross their desks weekly, whose do they take more seriously? Uh-huh, the ones with stage experience. Doing theater is also a possible way to get discovered—some agents, managers, and casting directors attend plays to scout for new talent. And they do go to towns and cities all over the country.

Being in the game puts you on the "performer's circuit," around other talented people who may have show-biz connections. And performers are famous for sharing information and ideas. You'll not only learn more about the business, but you may just get a lead on who's hiring, who's in town, and who's scouting talent!

You'll have to start, of course, by being in school plays or performing with the parks and recreation department, the local Y, or the church or synagogue in your town. Did you know that Debbie Gibson was in *The Sound of Music* at her church? So was her lead guitarist, Tommy Williams. Neil Patrick Harris also performed in church—he sang while his dad played the guitar.

COLLEGE THEATER

There are several other nonprofessional theaters "up the ladder." Colleges and universities, no matter how small, often have theater departments. It's a good idea to get in touch with them. Perhaps there'll be a production that needs a young person, or perhaps they could give you some leads on where to look. Also, one day you'll be ready for college and if performing's still your goal, you'll want to go to a college with a great theater department.

College theater is where many big stars began—people like Tom Hanks, Elizabeth Perkins (*Big*), Melanie Mayron ("thirtysomething"), and Scott Valentine from "Family Ties." There's an excellent book on the market called *Directory of Theatre Training Programs,* by Jill Charles, that lists colleges and conservatories all over the U.S.A. with recognized theater programs. The book explains what degrees are offered, requirements for acceptance, what kinds of facilities the school has, and how many productions they put on each year. If you're a high school junior or senior whose heart is set on a show-biz career, it's a good idea to thumb through this one! (Info on how to get all the books and publications recommended is in Chapter 14.)

COMMUNITY THEATER

Community theater is another place for a young person to get experience. Most communities have groups that put on plays. Check your local papers for advertisements of productions, or if you go to a local play, check the program for information about auditions. Once you find a theater, call or write to see if there's a play with a role for a young person and find out how to audition.

Community theaters often use people who've never acted before. They exist because people in the community just love theater. Tom Cruise's mother started a community theater in a little town outside Ottawa, Canada.

Community theater is often not as polished as college theater, nor is it as professional as the other types we'll discuss in this chapter. It can be a lot of fun and an invaluable learning experience. But actors don't get paid and there may be no professional guidance. Also, terms of work may not be stipulated. Look before you leap into a local production. I heard one story about a young girl in rehearsal for a community theater play who was worked for twelve hours at a stretch without a break. She fainted and was then fired for fainting! It pays to investigate first!

DINNER THEATER

The next step up the ladder of professionalism is dinner theater, plays put on in restaurants. People paying for dinner and a play expect a more professional production than community theater—they usually get it. There are often roles for young people and it pays to find out if there are any dinner theaters in your area. As a teenager Tom Cruise performed in dinner theaters in New Jersey, so did countless other movie stars. Dinner theaters often produce musicals, so aspiring singers and dancers should call too. One thing to remember is that dinner theater performances are usually in the evening, sometimes in the late evening, and not always on weekends. That may be tough for someone still in school. Your parents may not want you out late at night, working. Just as with community theater, check out the working conditions and the people involved.

CHILDREN'S THEATER

It may seem that children's theater is not as professional as dinner theater, but that's usually not true. Good children's theater groups are often quite accomplished and the best ones have been in business for a long time. An advantage for you is that many of the plays put on by children's theater groups will need young people to fill the roles. Many plays are musicals and need people with singing and dancing talent as well. New Kids on the Block's Joe McIntyre, along with several members of his family, used to be part of The Neighborhood Children's Theater in Boston. His fellow New Kid Jordan Knight believes they're good experience. He says, "Get into a lot of local shows to get some exposure. You never know who's in the crowd."

Just as with community and dinner theater, the best way to find out about companies in your area is to ask around *and* check the local papers.

REGIONAL THEATER

Regional theater is the most professional and structured theater you can get into other than the Broadway stage in New York. The season for regional theater is generally from fall through spring. Summer stock is the division of regional theater that runs from June through September. Performers and all staff are paid and usually have contracts that spell out all details of their jobs. Many performers choose to spend their entire careers in regional theater. Others think of it as a final step before heading for a movie or TV career in New York or Hollywood. Every state has at least one regional theater company, and many have ten or more active groups.

Regional theater is tougher to break into than any of the others described so far. For one thing, there are very few roles for teenagers. And if there is a role, the producers usually hire an older person who looks young. Performers ready for regional theater have usually been working for years, and they're not about to be aced out of a role by someone less experienced and younger. Another problem with regional theater for the beginner is that most performers are in Actors Equity Association, the union for stage performers. You can't just join the union. You must have a job to join, but you can't get a job without a union card. It sounds like a Catch-22, but there are ways to earn credit toward getting into the union. If you're in an internship or apprentice program, you may earn credits toward Equity membership. Some regional theaters are non-Equity, which means you don't have to be in the union to get a role. By performing in many of these you also get credit toward your union card. The best thing to do is to contact the nearest Equity branch for a detailed explanation of their requirements. (Addresses appear in the last chapter.)

The best thing about regional theater, however, is that many of them offer two things that you can enter as a teen. These are apprentice programs and internships. Apprentices work at the theater, anything from painting scenery to performing "walk-on" roles. "It's called paying your dues," says the director of American Theater Works, Jill Charles. "Apprentices may get a small stipend, but are responsible for paying their own room and board—most are college graduates who've had some training already." The work that interns do is just as rigorous. They can usually get school credits for their hours at a theater. Sometimes they, too, get walk-on roles.

Unless you happen to live right near an active regional theater company, it means you must travel and live away from home. That's next to impossible if you're still in high school, but it is a goal to shoot for when you're older.

There is another possibility, however, and these are summer training programs. Many regional theaters offer courses to teenagers during their summer season. Other training programs, not associated with a regional theater, usually work the same way. There is a fee for summer training programs, and sometimes it's quite hefty, but they offer many courses, from acting, improvisation, voice, movement, stage combat, to all forms of dance, including modern, jazz, and ballet, to directing, video, lighting, makeup, scene painting, and more.

The way to find out about regional theater apprenticeships and internships is to let your fingers do the walking—through a guidebook called *The Regional Theatre Directory*. It lists companies in every state, who they hire, what productions are upcoming, who to contact about auditions, and *how* to contact them. *The Regional Theatre Directory* also lists many dinner theaters.

The way to find out about summer stock theater, and summer training programs plus where and when auditions are held is in yet another guidebook by Jill Charles, called *Summer Theatre Directory*.

STARS WHO PERFORMED IN REGIONAL THEATER
BEFORE GETTING FAMOUS

Debbie Gibson was in *Annie* at the Broadhollow Theater in Long Island, N.Y.

Jason Patric (Lost Boys) performed at the Vermont Shakespeare Festival.

Amanda Peterson started out as one of *Annie*'s orphans in Colorado.

Robert Sean Leonard (Dead Poet's Society) appeared at a children's theater in New Jersey as did *John Travolta,* way back when!

Max Casella ("Doogie Howser, M.D.") was a regular at theaters in New York.

Paula Abdul spent every summer between the ages of seven and sixteen traveling with Kids of America, a dancing and acting showcase group!

Staci Keanan ("My Two Dads") sang in community theater in Pennsylvania.

Jason and Justine Bateman perform in theater all the time. Their dad, Kent, is a director of plays.

Tempestt Bledsoe performed in regional theater in Cape Cod, Massachusetts.

ALYSSA MILANO TELLS
HOW SHE GOT STARTED

"When I was a little kid, I was always a ham. Whenever people came over to our house in Staten Island, New York I sang and danced for them. My dad's a musician and my mom's a fashion designer, but no one was thinking about me being in show business or anything. I started taking dance lessons when I was four, and then I took piano, flute, and music theory. Later on, I studied voice as well.

"For my eighth birthday, my parents took me to see the Broadway play *Annie* and that's when I got really inspired. I said to my parents, 'I could do that.' But they didn't exactly drop what they were doing and get me an agent or anything like that!

"What happened was that, two months later, my baby-sitter heard about open auditions for the second national touring company of *Annie* and just to keep me amused, she took me. I tried out and I was one of four kids chosen to play one of the orphans, out of the fifteen hundred who showed up. But they told me later that they didn't choose me for my singing ability. They picked me because I could concentrate.

ALYSSA MILANO

"I really wanted to do this, so my mom had to close up her shop and come with me. We traveled on the road with *Annie* for fourteen months, and it made me want to do this forever! When I got back home, I did other plays in and around New York City.

"I worked through agents in New York and started going out on auditions for commercials. It was hard because they kept turning me down for being too ethnic-looking. I was darker and "more Italian-looking" than most of the kids up for commercials.

"But eventually I did get some. I also got a part in a movie called *Old Enough*. Then, in 1983, I tried out for the part of Samantha in 'Who's the Boss?' I got past all the interviews and then I had to audition in front of the network executives and it was really hard. There were, like, seventy-five people in the room and there was this one spotlight, right on me. All these people, they did not laugh and they did not say one thing. They all had cigars. I felt like I was being put on display.

"Of course, I did get the part in 'Boss' and since then I've been in other feature films, TV-movies, and even made my own exercise video. I've released an album in Japan and may do one here, too.

"I haven't had a lot of problems, at least not with school. I've gone to a private school and didn't think the kids treated me any differently. We moved to Los Angeles in 1985, and although I don't have a lot of girlfriends, that's okay because I seem to get along with boys better anyway. Of course, some guys that I'd like to be more than friends are too intimidated to come over, because I'm well-known. It upsets me when the tabloids print lies about me, but I guess you have to accept that.

"I love performing, there's nothing like making someone laugh. It's like a natural high. I'd like to star in a major motion picture, that's been one of my goals. I have tried, but either there's nothing good written for someone my age, or the part goes to someone else. I intend to go to college. That's real important because there are a lot of child actors who don't make it. So I want to go to school, then come back into the business after four years and do a really big movie, a comedy, or a drama.

"I got started because I was in the right place at the right time, but if you believe in something, my advice would be to never give up, to keep trying to fulfill your dreams. You never know until you try."

CHAPTER 6

ALL ABOUT AUDITIONS

An audition is a tryout. In the acting world, they're also called interviews. Many performers, hundreds or sometimes even thousands, try out for every single professional role. Being up against so much competition sounds scary—and it is! It helps to remember that every single one of your favorite stars has had to go through the audition process time and time again. And as you'll soon see, for every job they got, there are at least thirty others they didn't get! Everyone's nervous going into auditions, no one really likes to go—but they are necessary.

To understand how most acting auditions work, it helps to first see the "big picture," the step-by-step of how a role gets cast. It's a pretty complicated process!

1. The writer creates a character and discusses it with the producer and director of the TV show, movie, or play.
2. Casting directors are briefed and instructed to find the right performer to fit the role. They'll

be told, for example, "Find us a thirteen-year-old Dustin Hoffman." John Cusack was cast in *The Sure Thing,* when the call went out for "a teenage Tom Hanks." It's the job of the casting director to give the producer and director several choices for each role.

3. Casting directors give the character description to a "Breakdown Service," which writes it up and wires it to agents and managers.

4. Agents then decide which of their clients best fit the description and send photos to the casting directors. Most agents send pictures of *several* of their clients for the same role.

5. Casting directors let the agents know who they want to see and then audition each of the performers.

6. Each performer is evaluated. The ones who weren't right are eliminated. The actors they want to see again are "called back" for a second interview.

7. Those who make the first "cut" then audition for the director and producer. At that point they may be put on video or screen-tested.

8. More candidates are eliminated. Those left must meet and audition for the head of the production company. Often, they must also screen-test with the other actors, to see if they work well together. At this stage, the star of the TV show, movie, or play may get to approve—or nix—the candidate.

9. Then, if it's a TV show, the candidates must audition one more time, for the network executives. If it's a movie or play, they try out in

front of the executive producer (the person who's financing the project) or head of the studio. The big bosses have final approval!

At each of these steps, performers are eliminated. You can see why auditioning is such a nerve-racking procedure!

What I just described is the way most acting auditions work. But there are other ways casting directors find performers.

THE OPEN CALL

You've probably heard of the open call. That's the kind of audition where you don't need anyone to represent you in order to try out. Open calls are held all over the country. You usually find out about them in your local newspaper, on the radio, or in any show-biz trade publications (they're listed in Chapter 14).

Casting directors admit that open calls are usually held for publicity purposes—they don't really expect to find talent. But every once in a while, they do! Alyssa Milano's career got started when she went to an open call for a road production of the play, *Annie.* Jesse Borego, a dancer on the TV show "Fame," was discovered at an open call. Teen superstar Corey Haim got his first movie role by going to an open call for the movie *Firstborn.* Thomas Wilson Brown, of *Honey I Shrunk the Kids,* was discovered at an open call he read about in his local Santa Fe, New Mexico, newspaper. It asked for an eleven-year-old who could ride a horse. Tom was—and he could. He got cast in the movie *Silverado* from that ad.

The most famous open call of all, perhaps, was the one held in Boston in 1984. It netted all five New Kids on the Block, starting with Donnie Wahlberg!

Open calls usually work like this: You show up at the appointed place and find there are several thousand others already in line! Casting directors periodically scan the line. Some will bluntly tell people to go home—they won't even bother to audition them. It sounds cruel, and it *is,* but if they've advertised for a particular type, say a young teenager, and people clearly out of that age range show up, they will probably dismiss them. Other casting directors say they audition every single person who shows up.

Bring a recent snapshot of yourself to the open call, along with your resume. If you haven't got a resume, at least put your name, and your mom or dad's business phone number, your height, weight, hair and eye color on your photo. At some open calls, you'll be given a number and a card on which to write your vital statistics. They may also take a Polaroid of you.

Bring whatever else is asked for in the advertisement. Singers may be asked to prepare a song—dancers to have a routine. Musicians will probably be asked to bring their instruments, unless, of course, they play the piano! That should be provided. Aspiring actors may want to dress somewhat like the character description, but whatever you do, don't go overboard. It's hokey and casting directors know it.

Open calls are very stressful—expect to wait for hours!

When you're finally called in, you'll be auditioning

in front of several people. You may be videotaped at the same time. Actors will be given something to read. Singers may have to do thirty seconds of a song. Dancers may be grouped together and expected to learn a new routine in ten minutes flat!

After you've waited for hours, done your bit in what'll seem like a split second, you go home. If by some miracle casting people are interested in you, they'll notify you. In most cases, you never hear from them, but you never know until you try. If nothing else, open calls are good experience!

TALENT SEARCHES

Another kind of audition is a talent search. That's when casting people are looking for very specific types and will go to certain places around the country to find them. They don't advertise to the general public, as they might in an open call, but instead make contacts in specific places. For example, in the movie *Lord of the Flies,* producers wanted real kids (not professional actors) who looked like cadets. Casting directors scoured military schools and even boy scout camps.

Where talent searches are held largely depends on the movie or TV show being cast. For a movie like *Desert Bloom,* which takes place in a rural area, casting directors concentrated their talent search in the Midwest. Actress Annabeth Gish was discovered in such a search in her native Iowa.

Sometimes, casting directors don't actually go to all these places, but only call local agents and drama schools for videotapes of their young hopefuls. "Tape has been a real boon to the casting industry," say

Janet Hirshenson and Jane Jenkins. "You really get to see a lot more talent that way, it's faster and more efficient." The young boy who played Steve Martin's son Kevin in the movie *Parenthood* was discovered when his mom sent in a tape of him!

Other talent searches are specifically targeted at performing arts schools all over the country. Casting directors will routinely call schools in different states and ask if any talented teens might want to submit a tape of their work.

AUDITION DOS AND DON'TS

The way most performers get cast, however, is at an audition that's arranged through an agent. Here are some dos and don'ts on preparing for one of those:

DO pick up a copy of the material you'll be auditioning with well in advance. Your agent should supply it. You'll never be given an entire script, just the scenes you'll be reading. These scenes are called "sides."

DO learn as much about the story and the character as possible. That's the best way to get a beat on your character.

DO be on time! That's the first sign of professionalism.

DO be reliable. If you need to change your appointment, give everyone involved plenty of advance notice.

DO read out loud daily! Sometimes, you won't have the benefit of sides to study and you'll have to "cold read" something. Do it well and you're way ahead of the competition!

DO try to develop "a personal relaxation technique

that works for you," says Warner Brothers casting director John Levey. "If you're a nervous wreck, you'll never give a good reading. Loosen up!"

DO dress like the character—up to a point, that is! If the part's for a wealthy preppy, put on a sweater, skirt, or nice slacks and loafers. If it's for a street kid, get out those tattered jeans! Sara Gilbert knew the part of Darlene Connor on the TV show "Roseanne" called for a tomboy, so she wore her basketball uniform to the audition. Going overboard can be counterproductive, though. Jason Hervey, of "The Wonder Years," once auditioned for the part of a wacky teen in the movie *Down and Out in Beverly Hills.* Jason went in dressed sloppily and acted like a real loon. The casting director thought Jason was just plain crazy and didn't call him back!

DO "bring your real personality with you," say Jane Jenkins and Janet Hirshenson. "We're looking for *your* specific quality."

DO go in, do your best, and then forget about it!

DON'T buy a new outfit just for the occasion.

DON'T go to the hairdresser just for the interview.

DON'T look too sophisticated—easy on the makeup!

DON'T rehearse with your mom! She may try to help by telling you how to read a line. Do it *your* way, or practice with your sister instead.

DON'T act desperate. "That scares people," says Meg Liberman.

DON'T be cutesy. Casting director Paul Ventura remembers a young girl who'd given a terrific reading. She just about had the part nailed down when, as she was leaving, she turned to the director and in the most saccharine way said, "Now don't y'all forget me, my name is Susie Q!" At that moment she totally blew it. No one wanted to hire her for anything!

DON'T beg to "do it differently."

DON'T say, "When am I going to get a callback?"

DON'T say, "Did I get the job?" This is a turn-off to casting directors.

DON'T call them—they'll call your agent!!

WHAT TO EXPECT AT AUDITIONS

Okay, so you're totally prepared. What's the scene going to be like when you walk in for your audition? For the most part, auditions are held in a casting director's office. You'll arrive there—on time!—then you will be seated in an outer office and will sign in on a sheet provided. Yes, there will be other people there, but if the audition isn't for a commercial, there probably won't be as many as you think. Expect to wait, although casting directors try not to keep you too long. When you're called to meet with the casting director, you go in alone. Nine times out of ten, you'll start your audition by just chatting. There are two purposes for this. The casting person really does want to get to know you. She also wants to see you switch from being you to the character! Then you'll do your reading, with the casting person "playing" the other parts.

After you've finished, you'll be thanked and sent home. Rarely does a casting director give any indication of how you did. "Once in a while, if a kid gives a really blow-out reading, I tell him or her," says DeeDee Bradley. One clue that they liked you is if you're asked to hang on to the material—a sign that they're thinking of calling you back. Generally, however, you don't have a clue about whether you're in the running.

Music and dance auditions are a little different. They're usually held in a studio and accompaniment is almost always provided.

Almost all auditions for teenagers are held after school—usually between four and six o'clock.

If and when you're called back, your next reading will be in front of the director and producer of the project. You'll probably be videotaped at that time. A tip: Wear the same outfit you wore to the original audition so they'll recognize you.

Expect to see up to six people in the room for that second tryout—everyone's got an assistant!

After that, you go up the ladder and, as you know, at each step you'll either be eliminated or, eventually, you may just get the part!

WHY YOU DIDN'T GET THE PART

Of course, you may not get the part. Chances are, you won't. And there are hundreds of reasons why. Here are the most common reasons, all given by Hollywood's top casting agents. They may seem silly to you, but all are real!

You just weren't good! Which happens on occasion to the best of 'em. Heather Locklear remembers one audition she and a young Tom Cruise did together. "I was really bad," Heather later admitted, "and Tom wasn't as good as I was!"

You need more training. That's something your agent should tell you.

You were good, but somebody else was better. Happens all the time!

You gave the best reading, but someone along the line simply "liked" someone else more. 'Tis tattled that Tommy Howell did not give the strongest reading for the movie *The Outsiders,* but the directors thought he had the perfect look. They simply liked him better than actors who'd given stronger auditions!

Your look was wrong. Nothing you can do about it!

Your age was wrong. Ditto.

Your eye color was wrong! Double ditto.

You didn't look like part of the "family" already cast. When putting a "family" together, casting directors honestly try for similar physical traits.

You were: too tall, too short, too thin, too heavy, heavy but not fat enough, too blond, too dark, too . . . fill in the blank!

You were perfect, but the next person reminded the director of his daughter!

R-RATED: COPING WITH REJECTION

Going in knowing all the possible reasons why you didn't land a role should help you cope with feeling rejected. Often, however, it doesn't. It may help to realize that you are never auditioning in front of the "enemy." Casting directors want you to do well, they hope you are the one who gets the job. In fact, everyone's rooting for you because once you've been chosen, their job is done. And if you're good, it's good for them. "We're really on your side," say DeeDee Bradley and John Levey.

It should also help to realize that casting directors are people with incredibly good memories—that's practically a requirement for the job!—and even though they may not have picked you for one role, they will remember and request you when another comes up that you are right for. Tommy Puett is the young actor featured as Tyler Benchfield in the TV show "Life Goes On." He'd been auditioning and losing parts constantly. But when Tyler came up, DeeDee Bradley knew he'd be perfect for the role. She sought him out, and he got it!

To help cope with feelings of rejection, you really do need a strong self-image and a good support system of people who believe in you. For every audition, you must try to feel good about yourself. Always remember, as agent Helen Garrett says, "There are one hundred agents in Hollywood alone who handle teens; they've probably submitted five hundred photos for each role—and only one person can get the job. Don't take it personally."

Judy Savage expounds, "Okay, you cry. But you must be able to forget about it and go on to the next interview." Diane Hardin puts it succinctly, "Auditions are like buses—another will always come along. If you missed one, you'll catch the next!"

HOW THE MOVIE STAND BY ME GOT CAST

Janet Hirshenson and Jane Jenkins:

"That movie was one of the toughest we've ever cast. After four months of intense auditions and screen-testing, we came up with twelve teens, three possibilities for each of the four main roles. At that point, the decision was made by the chemistry between them and by who looked the most like the actors playing the parents. It was heartbreaking to have to tell somebody fabulous that he didn't make it after all that time. River Phoenix and Wil Wheaton, we just knew right away, they were brilliant. River tore your heart out with his first reading. Wil was equally as moving. Ethan Hawke, who's famous now for *Dead Poet's Society* and *Dad,* was up for Wil's role. It was an agonizing decision choosing between the two of them."

THE ONES THAT GOT AWAY

Here are some roles your favorite stars tried out for, but didn't get!

Fred Savage auditioned for the lead in the movie *Clara's Heart.* It went, instead, to *Neil Patrick Harris.*

Staci Keanan auditioned several times for a costarring role on the TV show "Kate & Allie," but she was rejected for being too young. She also traveled hours from her Pennsylvania home to New York City several times to land a role in a TV movie called *The Dollmaker* that starred Jane Fonda. Just when she was pretty sure she had it, the directors decided to use "real Appalachian kids" and not actors.

Jeremy Licht really wanted the role in *Stand By Me* that *Wil Wheaton* won.

Wil Wheaton was up for a lead role in *The Goonies* and the part of Sam in *The Lost Boys* that eventually went to *Corey Haim.*

SO YOU WANT TO BE A STAR!

Corey Haim tried out for the role in *Goonies* that went to *Corey Feldman!* "We were always losing out to each other," Corey Haim remembers. More recently, *Corey Haim* lost out on roles in *River's Edge* and *Dead Poet's Society.*

Sara Gilbert once quit show biz for three years because it was so disheartening! Another time, after five callbacks, she thought she'd gotten a part on a "Facts of Life" spin-off. She didn't, but the show didn't go anyway.

Jay Ferguson ("The Outsiders") was nearly inconsolable when he didn't get a role on the TV sitcom "Molloy." He'd been trying for three years without nabbing one role! He didn't quit, though, and soon landed the lead in "The Outsiders."

Paula Abdul just about had the TV series "Dirty Dancing" in the bag, when better-known choreographer Kenny Ortega decided to do it.

How do the stars cope with rejection? What advice do they have for you? Here's what some of them said.

Staci Keanan: "I remember that I always hated auditions, I never wanted to go out on a call. I was this little kid, driving around with my mom and sister, whining, complaining, and feeling tired all the time! But I didn't feel really bad about not getting jobs. I never thought it was because I wasn't good. It never bothered me. A lot of times you are just plain bad, but they don't tell you."

Jeremy Licht: "If I didn't get something, my attitude was that 'there's always something better around the corner.' For 'The Hogan Family,' I had to audition seven times!"

Jeremy Miller: "I went on three hundred fifty auditions in the space of a year and a half—and I never got a thing! Finally, I got 'Growing Pains.'"

Tommy Puett: "You cope by trying to make yourself feel better. Hey, I've interviewed for so many movies and haven't gotten one yet. I came so close . . . !"

Corey Haim: "My feeling is, if they want to reject me, it's okay. If someone doesn't want to take me, it's okay. I tried my best, I wasn't the right person. I usually just say to them, 'Sorry, and thanks for seeing me.'"

TIPS FROM THE EXPERTS

"It's not you they're rejecting. Hundreds try out, only one can get the part."

—Agent Judy Savage

"Go in with the attitude of making the casting directors comfortable. And *listen.* Sometimes I'll choose one person over another because he turned his head when I directed him to and the other person wasn't listening.

"Don't get discouraged if you're sitting in the waiting room and see people who are more well known than you are. Don't feel, 'Oh, God, why am I here?' Remember that casting directors love to see new people, especially if they're prepared and talented."

—Casting Director Paul Ventura

"Come in, do the best job possible, and go on to the next interview. If you're good, you'll get your share of roles."

—DeeDee Bradley and John Levey

"Luck is when preparation and opportunity meet. If you're not prepared, when opportunity comes, luck will slip through your fingers."

—Diane Hardin

STARS TELL: "THE WORST AUDITION I EVER HAD . . ."

Brian Bloom: "It was on a TV project. I was at the point where I just about had the job, I was at the last step of auditioning, for the network executives. I was up on a stage in front of an audience full of men and women in suits. I had just finished reading when someone yelled out, 'Take your shirt off.' I was shocked. I wondered, 'What's this got to do with me getting the job, with the success of the show?' I refused." (P.S. The show didn't go.)

Staci Keanan: "There was one time I was up for a singing role. I went in and suddenly realized that everyone in the waiting room, all the mothers and kids, were standing right outside the door listening and talking about who the best singer was. It upset me and messed me up so much, I forgot the words."

Jason Hervey: "Usually, if you don't get something, they don't tell you in front of other people. This one time, it was between me and this other kid. We were both in there together when one of the directors suddenly said, 'Okay, Jason, you can go. Paul, let's go to wardrobe!' I felt bad enough, this was like rubbing my nose in it!"

Wil Wheaton: "This happened when I was a kid, about nine or so. I was doing a commercial for brownies. I had to keep eating one brownie after another. Naturally, I got thirsty and kept drinking water. Well, I drank so much, I had to make a lot of trips to the bathroom—they fired me!"

Tommy Puett: "When I was waiting to read for Tyler Benchfield, I saw Chad Allen come out of the interview. I thought, he's so popular, they're going to give it to him. And I felt terrible because I knew deep in my heart that I was so right for this role. After I read, I went home and was so depressed! I thought, 'I'm never gonna get it, I'm never gonna get ahead in this business.' I threw my script out the window!"

Candace Cameron: "I remember this like it was yesterday, even though I was eight when it happened. It was a windy day and I had really bad chapped lips. The casting director looked at me and said, 'Honey, go back outside and tell your mother to wipe the lipstick off.' I told her I didn't have any lipstick on, it was just chapped lips, but she wouldn't believe me. She kept saying, 'Yes, you do. Now go wipe it off.' She had me in tears!"

Bronson Pinchot: "I had just broken up with a girl I really loved and I was really hurting. I had to go and sing this song about being in love and put a lot of meaning in it. The worst part was, the audition took place right next to the place she was living."

SO YOU WANT TO BE A STAR!

Corey Haim: "It was for *Over the Top*, the Sylvester Stallone movie. He told me I was too tall and I knew it. I kept trying to duck down and look smaller, but it didn't work. They laughed me right out of the office."

STACI KEANAN'S

ROLLER COASTER RIDE
TO TV STARDOM

"My mom says that when I was two and a half, I was entertaining people at McDonald's and Burger King, whether they liked it or not! At one place where I was singing and dancing, they actually thought I was the floor show. I remember that I just loved to perform in front of people.

"I took ballet lessons in my town of King of Prussia, Pennsylvania, but there were too many kids in the class, so I dropped out. Then my mom heard about a charm school where they taught you to twirl a baton and walk on a runway. Mom thought I'd like that, so she signed me and my older sister Pilar up. It was fun, and we met other kids who also liked performing.

"When I was four, a big talent pageant came to town. It was just for kids and one of the categories was 'Most Photogenic.' Mom sent in our pictures and we both took top honors in our age group. That's when Mom put it all together. She felt if we were that photogenic and we also loved to perform, maybe we had a chance of making it in show biz. So in the very

STACI KEANAN

beginning, this whole thing wasn't even my idea—but I'm glad we did it.

"My mom had no connections at all (unfortunately, my dad wasn't supportive), so she used common sense to start. She called up department stores in nearby Philadelphia and asked where they got kids to model in their catalogs. She also asked about good professional photographers. She had composite pictures taken of us and sent them to various agencies. She didn't get any response! Finally, she called one, Midiri Models, and asked if they were interested. They said, 'Oh, yeah, send us twenty more photos!' So my mom had to invest more money getting copies made up. Anyway, Midiri started sending us out and we began posing for print ads. Pretty soon, the agency got us started on local commercials. I found I liked it a lot and people were telling us that we should really try our luck in New York.

"By this time, my parents were divorced, so it was just Mom, me, and Pilar. New York was two and a half hours away, but we made the trek to see about getting representation there. The first agent we went to didn't work out, but then we signed up with Fox/Albert Management and they were great. They started sending me on auditions, but it was really hard because we were still living in Pennsylvania. There were so many days we'd leave school early, travel up to New York, go on auditions—*not* get any jobs!—then make the long trip home.

"We decided to move to New York when I was eight or nine. For some reason, it wasn't any easier. Pilar and I were going to public school, Mom was working for our managers. It seemed like every day after school, Mom would pick us up and there would be interviews. They were like cattle calls and I hated it.

"One really bad day, when Pilar was twelve, Mom dropped her at this photographer's studio for a shoot and then took me to an audition. Well, the audition was like a zoo and we weren't going to get back to pick up Pilar on time. So Mom kept calling the photo studio to let them know. Anyway, by the time we got back for her, Pilar was gone! The photographer intimidated her by saying, 'Well, I guess I'll have to just sit here all night until your mother comes.' Poor Pilar tried to find her way home and got lost! Mom was in a panic. Everything worked out all right; Pilar eventually found her way home, but we couldn't wait to leave New York. Besides, it was getting very expensive. I can't tell you how much we spent on taxis, meals, clothes, everything you need to go on auditions.

"Of course, I was booking things, commercials, voiceovers, TV movies, and mini-series, and Pilar was doing lots of print work. I also did some community theater. All the time, too, I was taking lessons: tap dance, improvisation, voice, and always singing lessons. And those were expensive, too! It was so stressful that after three years we finally decided to either go back to Philadelphia and forget the whole thing, or try our luck in Los Angeles.

"We opted to go west, and pretty soon after we did, I landed 'My Two Dads.' It was like we were being rewarded for all we went through in New York! It's still stressful, being a young person in this business, especially with school. I'm in honors Latin, so I go early in the morning to be tutored, before work, and then one late night a week, too. But I love the chance to act, that's what I'm in it for, that and getting to meet new people and go places.

"My advice is to get experience first, to see if you really like it. Get training, do community theater. And beware of agencies and photographers who do nothing but just take your money. Be on the lookout for good representation!"

CHAPTER 7

THE WONDERFUL WORLD OF COMMERCIALS AND VOICEOVERS

Next time you flip on the TV, don't get up for a snack when the commercial comes on. Pay attention instead. You'll see that many teens and preteens turn up on TV ads.

Commercials are a fertile—and lucrative—breeding ground for aspiring performers. Not every young hopeful is "right" for TV ads, but many types are represented. "There is a definite youth market out there for certain products," affirms Paul Ventura, whose company casts between four hundred to five hundred commercials each year.

For some performers, getting into commercials is a goal in and of itself. Others use them as a stepping stone to a TV or movie career, and still others never consider getting into them at all!

Commercials are a world unto themselves. You may need an agent who specializes in them to get started (in some local commercials, that is not always the case). Once you have an agent, you'll need profession-al photos that are called composites. These are "composed" of different shots of you with different looks—hair up, hair down, glasses on, serious, smiling, etc. Commercials have their own requirements, advantages, disadvantages, and distinct audition procedures.

WHAT IT TAKES TO MAKE IT IN COMMERCIALS

Wholesome looks, personality-plus, a variety of skills, and great "cold" reading ability are what count most in commercials. Watch carefully, and you'll see that most of the teens are pretty fresh-looking, wholesome types of all races. As you study commercials ask yourself honestly if you'd fit in. That's a tough judgment to make yourself sometimes, but see if you can.

Kids who land commercials are, for the most part, naturally bubbly and outgoing because commercials are almost always positive and upbeat. Their purpose is to make the viewer like a product, and to have it associated with a happy-go-lucky, wholesome personality makes sense.

The more skills you have, the better your chances of landing a commercial. Once again, check out what's on the tube: You see teens in TV ads biking, running, swimming, skating, jumping rope, playing instruments, skateboarding, juggling, doing just about anything and everything! They weren't taught those skills once they were hired—they came in knowing them. It's the "can-do" kids who score in commercials!

Most important for nabbing a commercial, however, is your reading ability. You have to instantly interpret and present material you've never seen before. Cold readings are customary in the world of commercials. You really need to be a fast study and have a good memory, too.

PLUSES AND MINUSES

What's so great about commercials? Why would you—an aspiring actor, singer, dancer, or musician—want to be in those silly TV ads? For starters, they're fun, fast, good experience, and they're financially fruitful! Commercials are usually pretty easy acting assignments—for the most part you're "playing" a character pretty close to yourself. The situations portrayed are hardly ever complicated. Also, most commercials are shot in a day or two, and when you realize that you could earn thousands of dollars for a day's work, commercials can be pretty attractive!

But there are other, more practical reasons for a serious young performer to crack the commercial market. It's the way most youngsters get into SAG, the actor's union. In order to be hired for nearly all professional roles, you must be in that union—only you can't get in until you've worked in a SAG project or are a member of another union. Sounds like another "Catch-22"—except that you can be picked for a commercial without being in the union. Once you've completed the job, you can apply for membership. That, in turn, makes it much easier to get other work.

Commercials can be your first step up the show-biz ladder in another way, too. Think about it, your face and talents would be visible to every producer, director, writer, and starmaker in show biz! Yes, performers can get their "big break" because someone saw them in a commercial. Manager Jeanne Niederlitz tells the story of a big-time producer who was viewing videotapes of people trying for the lead in a very important TV movie. No one seemed right—until the tapes ended and the TV went back on. The producer thought the guy doing the commercial was absolutely perfect! He was called in and got the part!

Besides bringing yourself to the attention of industry bigwigs, doing commercials also helps you forge relationships with casting directors. Once they know you, they remember—and when the time comes that you're right for a big lead, they'll call!

There are some aspects of commercials you might not like. Commercials exist to sell products, and if you're in them, you're perceived as the "spokesperson" for that product. This doesn't sit well with everyone. River Phoenix started his phenomenally successful career with a couple of commercials, but quit almost immediately because River, a strict vegetarian, didn't believe in the products he was endorsing. Although he stood to lose a ton of money, River followed his conscience and only appeared in four TV ads.

Another "problem" with endorsing a product by appearing in a commercial is that of "exclusivity." Once you're hired to represent something, you can't be in an ad for a rival product. In other words, if you're in a commercial for Coke, forget about auditioning for any other soft drink! If your face appears in an ad for Chevrolet cars, you can't nab the lead in one for Ford.

Sometimes, commercials are shot and you're paid for the day's work, but when the ad finally runs you've been cut out of it! Or, just as bad, many ads are filmed and then are never aired! Paul Ventura explains, "It happens all the time. Maybe the company for whom the commercial was shot just got bought out. Maybe someone at the top of the executive ladder simply didn't like it. There are a hundred reasons why you may go on a slew of auditions, finally land a commercial, and then it never runs." In that case, you'd get paid for the day's work, but that would be all!

COMMERCIAL AUDITIONS

Auditioning for commercials is a completely different game, too.

You go on many more auditions than you would for any other kind of performing role. It's common for a teen new to the business to go on sixty-five auditions before landing a single ad! "Commercials kids often go on three or four calls a day," says agent Carollyn DeVore. That means missing all afterschool activities if you pursue your career vigorously.

There's much more competition for each spot. Staci Keanan's mom, Jackie Sagorsky, puts it bluntly: "They're like cattle calls. Could be one hundred kids in the waiting room at one time. When you do get called in you get five minutes to audition—that's it." She's not exaggerating. Commercials casting directors routinely see one hundred hopefuls in two hours. A tip: Find out from your agent or the casting director as much as possible about the "character" and the product. Ask what you should wear. Casting directors are impressed with people who've made an extra effort.

A typical commercials audition goes like this: You arrive—either on time or early!—add your name to the sign-in sheet, and then pick up the "script." Since there are a multitude of others ahead of you, this waiting time is when you look it over and practice. In fact, that's what every other kid is doing, and that can be pretty disconcerting! Don't overpractice, say agents and casting directors. It's a sure way to ruin your naturalness.

Eventually, you'll be called in to a room to meet with the casting people and camera operator. Even though you'll just be chatting in the beginning of your five-minute interview, you'll be videotaped all the while. You'll be asked to read the script. Often, you'll be brought in with several other people who are also being considered for the commercial. You may be asked to talk to them while the casting director observes the chemistry among you and the camera gets various angles of you and the others. After approximately five minutes you're thanked and told to go home.

Within a week you'll find out if you're getting a callback. Commercials are cast rather quickly. Your attitude must be that if you get a call, great—if you don't, that's okay, too. "There are tremendous disappointments," Paul Ventura counsels, "only if you let them be."

Should you indeed land the commercial, your agent will say you "booked" it (that's the term used) and will inform you where and when to report. Usually commercials are shot in a day or two—almost always during school hours. You will need a tutor and welfare worker (or parent) on the set with you, even though it's only for a day. That's the law in California and many other states.

When you're finished, you go home, hope you don't get cut out—and pray they run it!

TRAINING FOR COMMERCIALS

As you can see, commercials require a specialized skill. As you'd expect there are classes geared especially for them. Taking cold reading classes and specific commercials workshops are good ways of preparing. But before you sign up for any courses, don't forget to investigate first! Talk to teens who've been through the course to find out if it helped them land jobs or auditions.

If you don't live in a major media center, you may be throwing your money away on a commercials workshop. But you might be in a better position to get "on-the-job training." Many commercials are shot regionally and routinely hire local talent. The way to find out about cracking the local commercials market is to call your local TV, cable, and radio stations. Ask for their advertising departments and inquire about how they get performers for their ads. You could have the beginnings of a career right under your nose!

VOICEOVERS

Voiceovers are especially attractive to teens. A voiceover is used in a commercial—or even better, in an animated feature—and only your voice is heard. You aren't seen. No, they're not glamorous, but as manager Diane Hardin explains, "Most kids love to do them. They're fun, you sit cross-legged on the floor with a bunch of other people and read. You don't have to worry about getting there three hours earlier for the hairdresser, makeup artist, and wardrobe person!" Looks don't count at all in voiceovers, only the quality of your voice and your ability to "act" a character with only your voice. And, yes, there are voiceover coaches!

The pay is great—in fact, many adults you've never seen make a wonderful living just doing voiceovers. John Travolta's sister Ellen used to do them, which was how John first got interested in show biz! Famous people do 'em, too. Surely you've recognized the voices of many stars on commercials, and on TV cartoons and movies. Teen star Christopher Daniel Barnes was the voice of Prince Charming in the recent Disney animated feature *The Little Mermaid.* Tiffany can be heard as the voice of Judy Jetson in the full-length animated feature *The Jetsons.* Tempestt Bledsoe began her career in Chicago doing voiceovers and radio jingles.

A distinct advantage of doing voiceovers is that you don't have the exclusivity problem. You can be the voice in TV and radio ads for five different cereals and then "play" Peppermint Patty in the latest Charlie Brown TV special!

There's a lot of work in voiceovers, especially since more and more G-rated animated feature films are being made. The one major disadvantage is the competition. "Casting directors tend to stick with the same kids over and over again. It's a tight market," reveals Jeanne Niederlitz. Where casting directors are always on the lookout for new faces, they're usually not looking for new voices. Also, many adults can sound young and are often hired to do kids' voices. The actress who played the teenage lead in *The Little Mermaid* was twenty-seven at the time! Don't let that discourage you, however, for once you do crack the voiceovers market, you could be set financially to pursue other kinds of performing work!

TEMPESTT BLEDSOE
From Commercials to Cosby — to College!

Tempestt Bledsoe is ten inches taller now than when she first started playing Vanessa on "The Cosby Show"—back then, in 1984, she was a petite 4'10"; these days she stands a statuesque 5'8". Her stature professionally, however, is something no ruler can measure. At just seventeen years old, Tempestt is one of America's most popular and recognizable young actresses.

Tempestt Kenieth Bledsoe was born and raised in Chicago, the youngest child of Willa and Keith Bledsoe, both public school teachers. Neither had any notion about or connection to show biz in any way. Yet by the time tiny Tempestt was four, it was clear that their little girl had something very special —a talent, energy, spirit, and interest in performing that was so strong and obvious, they couldn't ignore it.

After doing some research, Willa walked Tempestt into one of Chicago's reputable talent agencies,

TEMPESTT BLEDSOE

known for their large children's department. The A-Plus Talent Agency saw hundreds of pint-size performers, but Tempestt was a standout. Sharon Wottrich, the agent in charge, recalls, "Tempestt was about five—and she was adorable. She had talent, sparkle, and confidence. Besides that, she was a good singer and quite a little actress. She had it all, and we fell in love with her."

Tempestt started by modeling clothes for department store catalogs. The photo sessions were often long and boring, but Tempestt was learning patience —and how to take direction.

She soon graduated to commercials, where her reading ability and dramatic bent served her well. Naturally, doing commercials meant she and her mom often had to dash from school early to go to auditions for parts—many of which Tempestt didn't land. Auditioning was a tiring, often frustrating process, but Tempestt's love of performing was only growing stronger, and the Bledsoes hung in.

In 1982 the A-Plus Talent Agency began to develop children as voiceover artists and commercial jingle singers—a select few kids were handpicked to be part of the program. Tempestt was a natural. She had a great voice, and because her parents would allow no slang in the house, she had no regional dialect.

Tempestt loved voiceovers and jingles. For one thing, she didn't have to do much "in person" auditioning—tapes she'd made were shopped around by her agents. If Tempestt landed a job she had only to go to a recording studio. She didn't have to get dressed up or leave school early. The whole process took a lot less time than making commercials—plus, she made more money. Tempestt sang jingles for Kellogg's Apple Jacks cereal and Good 'N Plenty candy, among others. She might, in fact, have stayed in Chicago, happily doing voiceover work, had not the call come from a California casting agency that Bill Cosby was looking for young actors to play members of his family in an upcoming TV series.

Tempestt was one of hundreds who tried out for the part of middle daughter, Vanessa, who, at the time, was described as "a very bright and outgoing girl who seemed to do everything right." Tempestt was perfect for the part. Even so, she had to go back five separate times to audition. It was stressful—but by this time, she was a pro of nearly eleven who knew all about auditions, waiting, and wondering. She also knew that nabbing *Cosby* meant moving to New York, a big decision.

As fate would have it, however, at the time *Cosby* was offered, Tempestt's parents had separated; her older brothers were pretty much out on their own. Moving to New York seemed possible. The biggest concerns were Willa's job and Tempestt's schooling.

For all during her early years in show biz, Tempestt was taught that her education always came first. She attended the Poe Classical School on Chicago's South Side and never missed an exam or an assignment; she maintained a straight-A average. Her mom continued to teach.

When *Cosby* came along, Willa, ever supportive of her daughter, took a leave of absence—she didn't quit right away, because no one knew if *Cosby* would be a success. Tempestt enrolled in New York's Professional Children's School. During the days spent actually taping the show, she and the other Cosby Kids had a private tutor.

"The Cosby Show," of course, was a smash hit and the number-one show on TV for many years. As Tempestt's own popularity grew, she had the opportunity to star in other projects as well, including TV movies of the week, and the acclaimed "Afterschool Special" *Amazing Grace*. Tempestt put her talents to work promoting exercise and good nutrition among her peers: She's been spokesperson for the Great Raisin Fitness Challenge and even starred in her own exercise video, *Looking Good: The Teen Fitness Program, Featuring Tempestt Bledsoe*.

Her commitment to important causes affecting teenagers is strong. Tempestt has spoken on behalf of the Just Say No To Drugs campaign. She once refused to star in a TV movie unless a scene depicting her character with a can of beer was deleted. As Tempestt candidly told *TV Guide* about the incident, "Actors should take responsibility for their parts. I never asked to be a role model, but it's a fact that I am one. I didn't want to send kids a twisted message." Tempestt got her way and received great reviews for NBC's *Dance 'Til Dawn* movie.

Her schedule is more hectic than ever, but schooling has remained her top priority. She's continued to excel academically, and upon her high school graduation in June 1990, she achieved National Merit Scholar status. This year, while continuing with her hit sitcom, she'll go to college—full time! Bill Cosby, a staunch supporter of education, will arrange her

Cosby Show schedule around her college courses. That, of course, sits very well with Tempestt, who plans on getting her degree in science or medicine. Of course, she'll continue to act and maybe even sing. Tempestt sees no problem in doing it all. She always has—no reason to stop now!

CHAPTER 8

MONEY MATTERS

It's easy to be dazzled by the big money numbers in show biz—("He's making a million dollars a picture!")—and the conspicuous consumption—("She just bought a fire-engine-red Porsche with an awesome sound system!"). But don't be blinded by the "green" (as in dollars). Yes, there *is* major money to be made in show biz, but the hard fact is that only *one percent* of all performers make $100,000 a year. A smaller percentage make more, but most earn only $5,000 to $8,000 annually. Plus, there's never an easy way to make big money. There are incredible expenses associated with a successful show-biz career. It's *easy* to get ripped off. Having lots of money can lead to all sorts of trouble. And finally, where the money goes once you've made it is at the root of horror stories you would not believe!

For every teen celebrity whose earnings are judiciously invested and put toward college, there's another who has been stripped of his well-earned security by the very people closest to him. Yes, money often brings out the worst in otherwise decent and loving people. No, I'm not going to name names, but this chapter should give you a basic understanding of the role money plays in show biz—from both ends!

WHAT IT TAKES TO GET STARTED

Ya' gotta spend some before ya' make some—but not nearly as much as you might think! There are some expenses you can't avoid, but there are also as many you can—and should!

In the very beginning there's only one thing you should be laying out money for—*classes.* Getting trained is your number-one priority at this early stage.

As you get a bit further along, you might add different kinds of classes: dance, voice, and music. And, of course, each one will cost you. At one point in her training, Debbie Gibson and her family were spending $150 a week on lessons!

You may decide to use the summer for training and go to a specialty camp. They are expensive, often several hundred dollars a week.

Before you have an agent, you should be getting experience in local plays on the community level. That's not an expense, but if there are franchised agents in your area, you'll want to invest in fliers to invite them to come to see you perform. Also you should have someone videotape every play you're in. It's good to have samples of you "in action." If you don't have a portable video recorder, you'll need to rent one and, of course, purchase some tapes. Be aware of these extra costs.

You might also be sending out photos and résumés,

which requires an outlay for supplies and postage. It can add up! So can phone bills if you're calling to check the references of schools and representatives.

If you advance to regional theater and start out as an intern or apprentice, living expenses will be your responsibility. Also you'll certainly want to save for college or a university with a good theater program!

You shouldn't spend money on photos—until you get an agent. When you do, a good set of photos should cost between $150 to $350, with a ceiling of $400. There's no need to spend more. And, of course, your agent or manager should suggest several photographers for you to choose from. Photos and classes, however, are an ongoing expense. As a teen, you're still changing. You'll probably need to update your photos yearly. But once again, this is not until you have an agent.

As your career advances you'll be incurring more expenses. You'll need clothing to go on interviews, you'll need to be properly groomed at all times. You may decide to have a physical trait corrected, such as buck teeth or a stutter. Debbie Gibson had a lisp when she was starting out. Her family had it corrected.

If you don't live near Los Angeles or New York, you may very well get to the point where a reputable, franchised agent suggests you spend the summer in one of those two cities so he or she can send you out on professional auditions. Many young stars have done that, and that's very costly because living and transportation expenses are your family's responsibility. You might also be invited out to Hollywood during the school year for "pilot season" (when new TV shows get cast). In that case, you'd also have to hire a tutor. You'd never go to these lengths, however, until you had a good agent and you'd already worked professionally.

One more expense at all stages is books and show business trade papers. Books, like the one you're reading, can be extremely helpful as guides. Trade publications like the ones listed in Chapter 14 keep you up to date on all that's happening in show biz and may also steer you to auditions and agents.

WHAT YOU SHOULDN'T BE SPENDING MONEY ON

As long as there are starry-eyed show-biz dreamers, there'll be predators who are skilled at separating them from their money. Scams and rip-off operations run amuck in show biz. Here's how not to become a victim:

NEVER, NEVER . . .
Pay someone to become your agent.
Pay someone to become your manager.
Pay someone to interview you.
Pay an agent or manager a fee before you've been paid for a job *they* were instrumental in getting you. After you've been paid, theatrical agents get ten percent, managers from fifteen percent to twenty-five percent, and music managers may get more.
Pay an agency to put your photo in their book or magazine. It won't get you into show biz! In twenty years of working with teen celebrities, I've never met one who was discovered that way!
Pay a fee to a company that charges to take your your photo, write your resume and send it to agents. You can do that yourself!

Pay anyone that promises to get you into show biz. There are no promises, no guarantees. It's that simple.

BEWARE OF . . .

Package deals and managers who teach and insist you sign up for *their* classes only, or insist you get photos from one photographer only. There are some reputable managers who are excellent teachers, but none will *insist* you take classes with them.

Classes that arrange to get you photos. That's a common scam.

Classes that are outrageously priced.

Photographers who charge in excess of four hundred dollars for a portfolio of shots.

Modeling and charm schools. There are so many that are not reputable that you *must* investigate. Call the Better Business Bureau and talk to people who've gone there. Modeling school is not the way to get into acting or performing of any kind.

Musicians who charge big bucks to help you make demo tapes.

Any solicitation you get in the mail. In almost all cases they're not on the up-and-up. Nearly all will tell you how much potential you have— and then, they'll charge you for photos.

WHAT YOU CAN EARN

Theoretically, the sky's the limit, but, realistically, there are some numbers that are fairly standard.

Don't forget that before you start making any money, you need a social-security number.

When you're first starting out, you'll probably be paid "scale"—the least possible dollar amount as determined by the union you're in, whether it's SAG, AFTRA, or Equity. Every so often, new union contracts are negotiated and scale rises accordingly.

This year, scale for one day's work in a *commercial* is $366.60. That's as long as your face is shown in the final cut of the commercial. If for some reason you're only shown from the back, your status is downgraded to that of an extra and you get much less.

With commercials, of course, there are "residuals." Every time a commercial airs in any part of the country, you get some money. The amount depends on whether the commercial is shown all over the U.S.A. or just in certain areas and also on how often it runs. One good commercial can net you about ten thousand dollars. If you do more than one a year, that sum can skyrocket.

Voiceovers pay approximately $145 per ninety minutes of work.

New actors who are starting out as regulars in a television series usually make around $1,500 per episode, depending on how many weeks the series actually runs. Actors who appear less frequently will be paid less per episode. If the series is a hit, the regulars can usually negotiate for more money. Actors who've been on a series for over three or four years often do very well, in excess of $10,000 per episode. The pay scale for being in a *movie* is pretty similar— you get paid per week of work.

Stage actors who are just starting out in regional

theater are paid per week. If the play they're in is governed by Equity, they must join and get paid whatever the minimum salary is, based on the type of play they're in. The pay may be a minimum of $400 per week whether they're in a lead or supporting role. Equity dinner theaters may pay as little as $250 per week, depending on the size of the theater. Salaries on Broadway in New York are much higher, but any play that's non-Equity pays significantly less.

How much can a *rock 'n' roller* make? That depends —each musician strikes his or her own deal. In general, you get paid for recording a song, lots more if you write and produce it (as Debbie Gibson does) and have the publishing rights to it. Naturally, you earn money for performances, too.

All the figures I've just thrown out are basic salaries —they increase as you advance up the show-biz ladder! Agent Vicki Light describes a best case scenario. "You get paid scale for your first movie, the second maybe twenty-five thousand. Two films a year would be considered great, really successful." Naturally, your agent does the negotiating for you and if you've got a savvy one, you should do well. Really hot young actors can command two-hundred-fifty thousand dollars per movie, but, as Vicki reveals, "It's a big, big step to get them from two-hundred-fifty thousand into the five-hundred-thousand dollar range. Most young actors don't make that jump."

Nevertheless, even a few thousand dollars a year, with the promise of more to come, is a tidy sum for a young person.

EXPENSES YOU NEVER CONSIDERED

As you can see, there's money to be made, but as your career progresses, there are new expenses—some you may never have considered.

Remember the chapter on auditions, where you found out you may have to go on thirty calls before landing a single job? Each of those auditions is going to cost someone something, including gas, tolls, parking, and wear and tear on the family car! Inevitably, there are meals eaten out between interviews, and those can add up, too.

A lot of time is spent auditioning—and if you're a young teenager, that time is not only yours, but your mom and dad's, too. Your parents will be giving up time spent on their jobs or household responsibilities. If your mom or dad is running around with you, who's cleaning, cooking, and taking your little brother to soccer practice? Other people may have to be hired.

Then there are union dues. In order to work professionally in show biz, you will have to join at least one union. A SAG card is required if you're appearing on anything that's filmed (all movies, most commercials, and several TV series as well). The current initiation fee is $796. That's a one-time payment. After that, there's a yearly sliding scale based on your earnings, anywhere from $85 a year up. AFTRA covers all work done on the radio or that's videotaped. Many TV shows are taped. Their initiation fee and dues are on par with SAGs. Equity's initiation fee is $800, with minimum dues of $70 per year plus a small percentage of your earnings.

Other unions you might conceivably have to join are The American Federation of Musicians, the American Guild of Musical Artists, and The American Guild of Variety Artists! Several multitalented performers pay dues to all of them—most are members of at least two unions.

Agents and managers fees combined may take thirty-five percent or more of your salary. That comes "off the top," before taxes.

And speaking of taxes, depending on your earnings, good old Uncle Sam gets his share. Up to thirty percent! A minor is taxed as a single taxpayer. Don't forget that at some point in your career, you will need to employ the services of an accountant, possibly a lawyer, and business manager as well!

If you're under sixteen years old, and you work in a TV show or movie in California, there's still another expense. Under state law, your parents must provide a guardian over the age of twenty-one to be on the set with you at all times. The guardian can be your mom or dad, of course, but if either of them can't be there, someone must be hired.

The state of California has a law to protect a percentage of the money you make performing. It is called the Jackie Coogan Law and requires that at least twenty-five percent be put away in a trust fund that cannot be touched until you're eighteen. This was enacted for your protection and is very important.

It doesn't take a mathematical genius to add it all up. It's possible that thirty percent of your income will go to taxes, thirty-five percent to your manager and agent, twenty-five percent into a trust fund, and a portion for union dues, accountant and lawyer's fees. That doesn't leave much!

SO YOU WANT TO BE A STAR!

It's important to keep organized records of every expense you lay out related to your career. This is for tax purposes. Keep and Xerox copies of receipts for everything—parking, gas, tolls, taxis, phone bills, tapes, supplies, and any other expenses incurred in your "business." It is called show *business* for a reason! It may get to the point where you need a computer to keep it all straight.

HOW MONEY IS USUALLY HANDLED

Assuming you get to the point in your career where money is coming in, there are several ways to handle it. Some are better than others!

In a perfect situation (which is unusual, but does exist) your earnings should be invested for your future. There's nothing to say you can't put more than twenty-five percent away in a trust fund. The most savvy teen celebs—those with honest, caring people around them—usually do. Many put away up to sixty percent of their net earnings. They may not have the Porsche when they turn sixteen or the Rolex watch, but they will have their college education paid for and some security for later years. "No one's on top all the time," says agent Iris Burton, "there will be dry spells where you won't get any work. Have something put away for a rainy day." In fact, if your money is invested wisely, you could end up with a lot more than you earned!

This is not to say you shouldn't have some kind of an allowance—after all, you did work for the money. Some celebs and their parents come up with what they feel is a reasonable amount for allowance and upgrade it periodically. It's critical to learn the value of money, to learn how to budget. It's a lifelong lesson!

In the real world, however, it is not always possible to give yourself a small allowance and put the rest away for your future. In many households your earnings might really be needed. What's more, you may want to contribute to the "family pot." It is, after all, a good feeling to help the ones you love. No doubt, if you've come this far, your family has helped, been supportive, and possibly even sacrificed for your career. It makes sense to give something back—as long as you're able to put something away.

Many of the teen stars I've come to know have used their earnings to help out. I won't use their names because the information is very personal and I would not betray a trust. But I will give you some examples. One girl, who was a regular on a TV series that ran for several years, paid all her single mom's household expenses, bought the groceries, and paid off the mortgage. A boy who played a recurring character on a TV show came from a poverty-stricken home—he supported his family totally. A very famous teen movie star supports a family of seven (his dad is disabled).

In none of these cases are the teenagers being exploited; all have a good sum of money put away for themselves and all recognize the need to help out at home.

There are many worst-case scenarios where young performers are exploited by the people they trust most. Their stories will never be told in public, but all are true. What's more, they all involve people you know, none of whom is more than twenty years old. What happened is that the parents of these kids took the kids' money, or all that they could get their hands on. "A lot of kids support their parents here in Hollywood," says manager Delores Robinson. "In some cases, I've seen the devastation that can cause."

One young TV star's divorced mom has been in and out of marriages several times. Each marriage has produced a child, and her working son pays every time. Another star's mom would have left him almost penniless when he turned eighteen if it weren't for a caring manager who put as much as she could in trust funds for him. In the worst case I ever heard of, a young movie actor was taken by both his parents, who were substance abusers. Very sick people, they used his money to pay for their self-destructive habits. Since the actor had been working since he was in diapers, it was a lot of money!

There are more horror stories. There's the one about the kid on a soap opera whose salary went directly to his manager, a family friend he trusted. One day armed with several thousand dollars of the kid's money, the manager skipped town.

A twenty-four-year-old actor had been working steadily in commercials, TV, and film since he was three years old. His mother had been handling his finances. Too late he found out that she'd never filed income taxes for him—the IRS came after him and said he was responsible for back taxes!

How can you protect yourself? Hopefully, you'll never find yourself in a situation where you're exploited. And I would never suggest that you defy or challenge your parents, no matter what any outsider thinks. A good agent or manager, whom you can confide in, should be able to help you set up trust funds or find out about any legal recourse you may have.

KIRK AND CANDACE CAMERON
A Family Story

"I never wanted to be an actor. I just fell into it," admits Kirk Cameron. He's not being modest—Kirk was just along for the ride when his mom took all her kids to see an agent.

The only reason homemaker Barbara Cameron did it was because a neighbor had sent the four Cameron kids' photos in to *her* agent, Iris Burton. The neighbor happened to be Fran Rich, whose son Adam was scoring in commercials and on the TV series "Eight Is Enough."

No one in the Cameron clan had any connection with show biz, even though they lived just outside Los Angeles. But daughter Bridgette seemed a born performer, and for that reason, Barbara acquiesced and went off to meet Iris, one of Hollywood's top children's agents. She certainly never thought Kirk would get into show biz; he was so shy. She only took him along so his feelings wouldn't be hurt!

It was surprising to everyone, then, when Iris Burton asked to sign Kirk up for a year and suggested that little Candace return when she was older. It was

KIRK CAMERON

CANDACE CAMERON

decided that neither Bridgette nor Melissa had "unique-enough looks."

Kirk, however, had a sparkle. Yes, the nine-year-old boy was shy and stiff, but the agent saw something in him. She felt confident he'd loosen up after a while.

Kirk almost didn't. He went back six times for his first commercial. During one interview he was so scared that he cried the whole time! Still, he began to land one out of every ten he went for, which is an excellent record. Still, it wasn't easy. Often when Barbara was picking Kirk up from school to take him on auditions he was tired, hot, hungry, and loaded down with homework. But they went anyway.

After a while Kirk got bored with commercials. He signed up for an acting workshop with Diane Hardin to prepare for movie or TV work, but he only went to six classes. He was natural enough, and it was decided that he wouldn't continue with the training. In fact, Kirk's had no other training at all.

He was cast in a movie called *The Best of Times,* and a short-lived TV series, "Two Marriages." When "Growing Pains" came along, it was truly Kirk's naturalness that got him the part of Mike Seaver. The producers really wanted a young-looking eighteen-year-old, so they wouldn't have to provide a teacher or welfare worker on the set, but when fourteen-year-old Kirk came in, they changed their minds. He was so natural that he cracked up when he read Mike's funny lines and won himself the role that made him famous.

Things didn't come quite so easily for Candace. For one thing, it is harder for girls to break in; plus there were a lot of other blond, blue-eyed cuties out there. And being Kirk Cameron's sister did not help, for Candace started when she was five, before Kirk got famous. Candace landed one out of every twenty commercials she went up for—and the very first one she got, for Mutual of Omaha, never ran!

"I never really cared for commercials," Candace confides. "You have to be so bubbly on auditions. I just felt phony." Nevertheless, she went on interviews for several years and tried not to let the rejections get to her. She landed the costarring role of D.J. in "Full House" when she was eleven.

Meanwhile, Kirk was having a tough time dealing with overwhelming fame. If he just fell into acting, he certainly never imagined success gone haywire, ten thousand fan letters a week, paparazzi camped on the front lawn, and the very real threat of not being able to live a normal life. It was doubly tough on Kirk because at fourteen and fifteen years old, he was going through an awkward adolescent stage and didn't understand why people were making a fuss over him. He never thought of himself as anything special or even as especially good-looking. He had a hard time coping with the intense adulation.

There were hassles with some of his teachers at school who didn't want to accept the homework he'd done at the studio. And it was hard to maintain his friendships. But Kirk graduated with his class and proudly points to the fact that his real friends are not part of the "Hollywood crowd."

There were other problems brought on by Kirk's superstardom. It wasn't easy for his middle sisters not in show biz. Extra effort's been made to encourage them in other directions.

At one point family pressures got so intense that Barbara and husband Robert Cameron separated for five months. Those were the tough times, but happily the family's back together now.

Kirk wants to expand into feature films. He's done two, *Like Father, Like Son* and *Listen to Me,* and though neither was a huge box office success, he's committed to future movie projects that are meaningful.

The Cameron family's advice for young hopefuls is "don't go into show biz expecting that you're going to be a star. Get into it because you love it, do theater. And if you do get into it, don't think of acting as the only thing in the world. It's a nice thing, but it should be part of your life, not all of it."

CHAPTER 9

ROCK 'N' ROLL,
MUSIC, AND DANCE

Debbie Gibson, Tiffany, New Kids on the Block, Paula Abdul, and Martika all broke into the music business in—or just past—their teen years. They, however, are the exceptions to the rule. Although Debbie's success at sweet sixteen paved the way for younger people to be taken more seriously in rock, it's still unusual for anyone under twenty-one to be signed by a record company. Most everyone on the charts has been at it for years—training, practicing, playing in tiny out-of-the-way clubs to apathetic audiences.

Whether you want to be a rock 'n' roll star, Broadway belter, ace guitarist, drummer, or the next dancing dynamo, you better know that it's not gonna happen overnight! Just as in the world of acting, there are dues to pay on the long and winding road to the top. Most of what you've read so far in this book about breaking into show biz applies to aspiring music and dance performers, just as it does to actors. In this chapter we'll get a little more specific about breaking into the music and dance world.

TRAINING

No one does it without *some* training: The most natural, melodious voice needs technique; the quickest pick-it-up-by-ear guitarist needs pointers; the most limber dancer needs to know all forms of his or her art.

Singers may train with a good voice teacher and perhaps, at some point, a vocal coach. No one can teach you to sing professionally, but a voice teacher should help you learn, among other things, proper breathing and relaxation techniques, and how to sing without pushing or straining your vocal cords.

To accomplish this, many voice teachers start with exercises that seem to have nothing to do with singing! When Debbie Gibson went for her first lesson with voice teacher Guen Omeron, she was stunned to be told, "All right, get down on the floor, we're going to exercise!" Guen explained, "In order to learn to sing properly, you must strengthen the abdominal muscles that support the diaphragm. It gives you the strength to sing a whole phrase without fading out or going flat."

Voice teachers should also instruct you in the proper techniques to counter the frequent problems singers have with sore throats and nodules that may form on their vocal cords.

Vocal coaches are not the same as voice teachers. "A vocal coach," explains Robert Marks, who is one and has worked with Debbie Gibson, Martha Byrne, Jon Cryer, and many young stars of Broadway, "helps the singer find songs (which isn't as easy as it sounds for a young person), creates arrangements for the pieces, and prepares the singer for auditions and actual performances."

Neither a voice teacher nor a vocal coach may be easy to find if you don't live in a major metropolitan area. If you're lucky enough to live in or near New York City, you can contact the New York Singing Teachers Association for recommendations of qualified professionals. Write: **Jeannette Lovetri, NYSTA, 317 W. 93rd Street, Apt. 3B, New York, NY 10025.** Otherwise, try the **National Association of Teachers of Singing, c/o Bob Downing, Executive Director, NATS, 2800 University Blvd. North, JU Station, Jacksonville, FL 32211.**

No matter where you live, you should always *ask* around. If you know people who have voice teachers, find out who they use and if they're satisfied. Robert Marks says, "Finding a voice teacher or a vocal coach is just like finding any other professional, whether it's a doctor, dentist, or a lawyer: Ask your friends, try to discover what the person's reputation is."

If you don't live near a large city, try contacting your local college or university. Professionals in the music department often give private instruction. The piano teacher who worked with Billy Joel is a professor of music at Hofstra University on Long Island, New York!

Before you sign up for lessons, however, find out what the teacher's background is: operatic singing, Broadway singing, or acting. That will give you an idea of the kind of instruction you're likely to get! Also find out who some other students are and call one or two of them. Finally give a call to the local

Better Business Bureau and make sure no one's filed a complaint against the person you're considering.

How do you know if you're actually getting anything out of your voice lessons? When you're a teenager, the voice lesson should be no longer than a half-hour. Done correctly, singing is strenuous exercise! You should never feel any pain, burning, or hoarseness after a lesson—instead, you should feel relaxed.

If you can't find a proper voice teacher or vocal coach, it's better to do without than to sign on with the wrong person.

That advice also goes for the aspiring musician. You need an instrument before you can go in search of professional instruction. To find a teacher, start by asking for recommendations at the store where you bought your instrument.

There are dance schools in just about every small town, and nearly all performers, whether they're aspiring dancers, actors, or musicians, often find them very helpful. Tap, jazz, modern, and ballet are the forms most often taken. Once you're a little further on in your dance training, you might want to research nearby ballet companies that may have schools associated with them.

Whether or not you're able to find professional training in voice, dance, or a musical instrument, there are things you can do at home to get ready for show biz.

Listen to the radio! You do that anyway, of course, but you should be listening to a variety of stations, with a critical ear. Aside from separating good music from bad, you should be savvy about what kind of music is selling.

Listen to records! But don't just concentrate on one type of record (rock, rap, pop)—listen to a variety of good music. Robert Marks feels that original cast albums of Broadway plays are often overlooked as excellent examples of good music.

Go to concerts! Hearing live music is a thrilling and inspiring experience. You may get some great ideas. Debbie Gibson said that by going to as many concerts as she did, she learned what makes a good concert, what turns the audience on. She's incorporated all that into her shows now!

Go to ballets and dance recitals! There's a lot to be learned by observing!

Study music and dance—learn about its history and theory. Learn to read and write music—it could be invaluable later. As you'll soon see, it's the songwriters and publishers who often make the most money in the music world!

GETTING EXPERIENCE

There's no substitute for performing experience and you should get as much as you can. The most obvious place to start is at school! Be in the chorus, glee club, band, orchestra, or dance club. Enter your school's talent competitions. Performing in school combines training and experience—plus, you meet other kids who are interested in the performing arts.

Sing in your church or synagogue choir, perform at school dances, parties, sweet sixteens, wherever you can. Try out for community and local dinner theater. Nearly every theater puts on a musical production and looks for singers, musicians, and dancers.

Forming a band with your friends is a good way to

get started. Just about every rocker on the scene today was part of a band in junior high school.

Once you're past school dances, the next step is getting experience in local music clubs. Find out what clubs are in your area, call up, and ask who books the talent. That's the person you'll want to audition for. Naturally, you'll want to check out these places before you agree to perform in them.

There are ways to be ripped off while getting experience. Some unscrupulous promoters will ask a band to pay in order to perform, the rationale being that you need the exposure they can provide. Stay away! Talk to others who've played in the venue before—that's always your best bet.

Keep looking for places to perform, ways to be seen. Robert Marks says, "When someone calls you for a legitimate performing job, just say yes! Do everything you can!" Sandy Einstein, who's worked with rock groups Journey and Mr. Big, concurs: "To succeed as a musician, you have to really want it—be *active,* not re-active!"

EXPENSES AND DEMOS

There are, of course, expenses along the way when a singer, musician, or dancer is getting started.

Naturally, you'll have to pay for lessons, and those prices vary depending on the type and frequency with which you take them. The best policy is to be a good consumer—shop around! The lowest-priced classes may not be the best; the most expensive may not be what you need.

For musicians, the price of your instrument can be a major expense. Many guitarists and piano players start out with secondhand instruments. Only when they can afford it do they go out and buy something new.

Demos—demonstration tapes—always interest singers and musicians. At some point in your career you will need to make demos as realistic samples of your best work. You'll perhaps need them to use as audition pieces to play in a particular club. You may need them to attract management or an agent. You will certainly need them to sign a recording deal.

Demos are often put together in a professional recording studio with musicians, arrangers, and engineers—all of whom must be paid! They can be a very expensive proposition and novices are ripe for getting ripped off. Some tips: If you are part of a band and you have experience, you've played locally to positive feedback, you may want to research sound studios in your area to cut a demo. Most studios have rate cards that tell you exactly what they charge and for what. Perhaps you don't need a lot of extra session players (musicians); perhaps someone in your band is knowledgeable about arranging and knows how to work a sound mixing board.

But you don't always have to go to the expense of renting a studio and paying professional musicians to get a demo made. Debbie Gibson used to make her own demos in her garage! And Robert Marks will help his clients get demos made right during their lesson. "Find the least expensive way to get a demo made," he counsels. "You shouldn't be spending thousands on them."

There are many unscrupulous characters who prey on young singers and musicians and offer—usually for a hefty fee—to get demos made for them. They claim to have contacts at record companies. Nola Leone, an executive at Curb Records in Los Angeles and a long-time music industry insider, advises, "If someone believes in you enough to offer to do a demo for you, let them pay for it." Nola further advises not to attempt demos until you are really polished. Most music starmakers are used to hearing professional-sounding demos—and don't send a demo of a popular song. "They've already heard it done professionally. By comparison you can't help but sound worse," says Nola.

Does it ever pay to send demos, unsolicited, to record companies? *Hardly ever* is the consensus of opinion. Record companies get tons each week, and while they do listen to all of them, most get tossed. Advises Nola, "It's better to send a demo to someone with real connections in the music industry than to send it blindly to a record company. Your real purpose in making demos is to get people interested enough to see you live. That's what you really want."

AGENTS AND MANAGERS

What part do agents and managers play in the music world? Pretty much the same as in acting. An agent's job is to find work for you—a manager's is to guide your career. All the same rules apply. Agents (most often referred to as booking agents in music) should be licensed by the unions and by the state; managers are not. Agents charge the standard ten percent after you've made money; managers are unregulated. However, there is some conventional wisdom about music managers—*most* reputable ones charge between fifteen percent to twenty percent of what you make when they've helped you land a gig. Some music managers have been known to take as much as fifty percent, however. Don't sign *anything* until it's been approved by a competent entertainment attorney who's working for you. It's the best investment you can make.

One major difference between music and acting representation is that you don't really need music agents or managers until later in your career. In fact, it'll be hard to get someone reputable to represent you until you've gotten some national exposure. Some of what an agent does—booking you into clubs and other venues—you can often do yourself. And good, solid, experienced music managers are hard to find, especially outside of urban music centers.

When you're at a point where you need a musical agent, finding one is similar to finding a theatrical agent. The unions, especially SAG, are a good place to start. Many theatrical agencies also have music divisions. Once you've tracked down potential agents, you'll need to send a demo tape or find some other way of getting them to see you live. This is where you make it or break it!

Is it ever possible for an agent or manager to discover you? Again, it depends on where you are. If you're in New York or L.A. and you're playing at a local club, of course, it's possible. The truth about the music business, even more so than in acting, is that at some point in your career, you will probably have to go to New York or L.A. Ideally, it will happen during or after college. What you do before you reach that stage is *prepare,* so that when you do make the move, you're absolutely ready to be discovered!

WHAT YOU CAN EARN

There's no base amount that singers and musicians earn as professionals, although there are certain hourly rates set for session players by the American Federation of Musicians. In general terms, you get paid for live performances, you may get something for cutting a record, and you get artist royalties when that record sells. All sums, however, are negotiated by your agent and the record company. Songwriters and publishers earn royalties whenever any of their songs is played on the radio. The major publishing houses, ASCAP and BMI, have systems that record how often songs are played and what the songwriter's share is.

If you've not only sung but also played on, produced, and written a song, you're in for a much bigger piece of the pie. That's why so many singers and musicians contribute original music to their albums.

Of course, going on a major tour can earn big bucks, but what most people don't know is that the artist herself picks up much of the tour tab. Sometimes it costs singers more to mount a tour than they ever make! They hope that audiences will go out and buy the record after the concert!

As with acting, union dues eat into your music earnings. Musicians may, at some point, have to join the American Federation of Musicians. Singers who perform onstage will probably have to join Equity and possibly the American Guild of Variety Artists. If you're on the radio, AFTRA is a must. And, of course, if you sing jingles in commercials or perform in a movie or TV show, it's SAG. Some well-rounded stars pay dues to five different unions!

No question that the music world is glamorous once you're in it, but the realities are tough.

ROCKER TIFFANY REVEALS HER TRUE STORY!

"I started singing around the house when I was about two years old. I loved to sing. I was inspired by radio. At the time, my mother and stepfather listened to country music. When I started to go to school, every day I'd come home and go practice in my room. If I got grounded, my mom used to make me sit in a corner facing a wall. Well, after a while, that was no punishment, because I'd sit there and sing to myself, figuring, okay, this is my time to practice! Mom got wise to that pretty soon and gave me something else to do, like the dishes.

"I loved to imitate any female singers I heard on the radio. It wasn't until I was ten that I broke away from country. I had an older cousin who listened to Fleetwood Mac and Heart, and my aunt would let me sneak in her room and listen to her records.

"And I found that I had a similar sound to Stevie Nicks, I could sound like her. And from that moment on, I decided I wanted to be a pop singer.

"My mother and stepfather began taking me around to local bands. Like if there was a fair, with a

TIFFANY

band, my stepdad would go up and say, 'Look I have a nine-year-old daughter who knows a couple of songs, if you'll just let her sing with you.' And that was great with me, I wasn't shy. I just wanted to sing. So I'd get up and sing a couple of songs. I mean, usually the band would hesitate at first, and then they'd say, all right, one song.

"I'd get up there and sing one song and they'd say, 'Well, do you know any more?' And after that I just started to have a little bit of a following because I'd work with the same bands over and over again. Whatever dates they got, they'd ask me to come along. We'd go down to San Diego—I'm from Norwalk, California—and sing every weekend. Once, we even *drove* all the way up to Anchorage, Alaska, for a gig that was set up for me. It took three days and my mom and stepdad had no sleep on the road. I had a date that I had to be there for. I remember arriving an hour and a half before I had to go on. I hadn't had a shower in three days! I just went into a rest room and I washed up and my mom had made an outfit and I got dressed and went onstage!

"When I started singing pop music, I just met people. It was a matter of luck, of being in the right place at the right time. After a while, I began doing demo tapes as favors for the bands. Like, they'd say to me, 'We're gonna record this weekend and if you could come in and do some harmonies, we'd really like that.'

"At the age of twelve I was recording with one of the bands at a studio run by George Tobin. He walked in and listened to someone playing back a vocal I had done. I guess he asked who was singing and someone said, 'That's that little girl over there in the corner.'

And I was doing my homework and George walked up to me. He had a guitar and he said, 'All right, do you know any Beatles songs?' And I said, 'Yeah.' He said, 'Well, sing this in this key.' After a while, he was playing, I was singing, and he said, 'I'd like to record you.'

So I recorded with George and he became my manager. But since my parents and I didn't know much about managers and we couldn't afford an entertainment attorney—a divorce lawyer handled my contract—I didn't get the best deal. Not that George wasn't a great manager, but if I were giving advice, I'd say get yourself a good entertainment lawyer, someone with experience, to handle your contracts, before you sign with anyone.

"Everything happened pretty fast. After I recorded with George for a year and a half, he called and said, 'I'm showcasing the album.' It was about six songs at the time, and he'd have record companies come in and I'd sing. He was trying to prove that it wasn't him behind a console, I really could sing.

"When George called and said MCA Records wanted to sign me, I was really shocked. I was most of all thankful, but shocked. It didn't hit me until I realized that all these bands I'd been singing with all these years never got signed. And they had families and all—it's *hard* to get a record deal. For me to just go in and cut an album and get a deal is pretty amazing.

"Awhile after the album was released, George called my mom and said, 'Well, what's Tiffany doing? I have some news for her.' My mom said I was doing the dishes. And I had the phone resting on my shoulder, and he said, 'I got good news for you. "I Think We're

148

Alone Now" just went to number one.' And all I could say . . . I mean, my heart started pounding, and I knew how great that was, but all I could say was 'cool.' I was thrilled to death, but all I could say was 'cool'!

"My advice for other kids who want a singing career is to get with your church choir and sing. That's good vocal training. You learn your range and how to exercise your vocal cords.

"And take the opportunity to sing whenever and wherever you can. I performed sometimes in front of only ten people, and I never got discouraged because, you never know, maybe there's a president of a record company out there on vacation with his kid or something. Do talent shows, get as much exposure as you can. I'm not trying to say go around your school and say, 'Well I can sing,' 'cause kids are going to be like, well, who really cares? But if there's something you can get involved in, go do it. Try to do the most you can without a manager.

"Taking voice training is good, too. I didn't take any early on, but I do now. I learned how to relax my vocal cords and, like, if I have a cold, how to throw my voice in a different place. A lot of times on the road there are different climates and they affect your voice. You have to learn how to take care of your instrument."

CHAPTER 10

PITFALLS: THE DARK SIDE

It's easy to see the highs of a show-biz career, but there's a downside as well. And none of the downside problems magically disappear when you become a star. In fact, they can become overwhelming, unless you know how to avoid the traps.

DON'T LOSE YOUR SELF-ESTEEM!

When you're first trying to get a foot in the door, you face rejection and rip-offs that can dash your hopes and dreams for good. If you've read this far, you know how much rejection there is in this industry. Take it to heart and you could lose the most important quality you need to get through life—self-esteem. For in show biz what you're "selling" is yourself, and if no one wants to "buy" your product, you could end up feeling like a failure as a person. A strong ego and an even stronger support system (from family and friends) are what you need to combat those self-destructive feelings.

It's critical to separate *yourself* from your career.

SO YOU WANT TO BE A STAR!

You are not what you do, or what you're trying to do! *You* are a good person, a kind, worthy, intelligent, talented person—no matter what you end up doing in life.

DON'T GET TAKEN!

The potential for being cheated is also strong in this business. There are unscrupulous characters just waiting to take advantage of you and your money. It can't be said often enough—don't be blinded by the light of your dreams. *Stay away* from anyone or any situation that makes you uncomfortable or is against your morals or ethics. As agent Vicki Light bluntly puts it, "You don't ever have to take your clothes off to be a star!" Make sure there's an adult you trust with you, or nearby, at all times. Keep your eyes and ears open, and don't believe everything people tell you. There are no promises in this business, there are no guarantees.

You will run into people who will bully and intimidate you, who will tell you that unless you do it *their* way, you haven't got a shot. Bull. Follow your own instincts. "To thine own self be true."

WRONG AGE? WRONG SEX?

The best time to break into show biz, say the experts, is either when you're six or after your eighteenth birthday. Cute or unusual-looking little kids are always in demand—most of the teen stars you know started when they were tykes. As a teen trying to break it, you're going up against kids who've been doing this all their lives. That's a tough nut to crack! Meg Liberman says, "I always have trouble casting kids to play opposite Fred Savage—he's so good and so experienced. It's hard to match him."

It's easier after eighteen for the simple reason that you are legally an adult, and studios don't have to hire a tutor for you. Being a young-looking eighteen-year-old is a definite plus. Here's a secret—nearly all the "teens" you saw on the show "21 Jump Street" were in their twenties! Same goes for "Head of the Class" and "Just the Ten of Us."

It's easier for boys to break in than for girls. Manager Jeanne Niederlitz states, "Seventy percent of the work in this business goes to boys and men." Look closely at commercials, TV shows, movies, and the music charts and see if it's not true. Men are still at the top of the industry, and they tend to hire their own sex.

IT'S OKAY TO CHANGE YOUR MIND

And, yes, in the end, you may very well have to face the fact that you may not make it as a performer. In spite of everything you've done, you may at some point decide to pack it in. How do you know when it's time to quit? Casting director DeeDee Bradley, who tried for years to become an actress, offers this advice, "If you're depressed all the time it's time to quit. If you go for interviews, but never get any callbacks, or never get any positive feedback, it's time to go on to something else. And you know what? That's okay. Not all of us were meant to be performers, but that doesn't mean you'll never be part of show biz. Some of us were meant to be directors, writers, agents, managers, publicists, producers, artists—and, yes, casting directors, too!"

PRESSURE AND COMPETITION

Becoming a performer doesn't mean you've successfully avoided all of the pitfalls. There's much to be aware of when you do finally get your career rolling!

The pressure is intense, the competition, unrelenting. "There's a lot of pressure to please, always to please other people," notes Diane Hardin. "And that's a real danger." The actor Harold Pruett of the TV show "The Outsiders" has been in show biz since he was a kid. He candidly reveals, "Most of my life was spent trying to please other people, and as a kid I couldn't distinguish between who I was and what I was doing. If adults told me I was good, I believed it. When they told me I did a bad job in a part, I thought I was a bad person."

How do you avoid feeling pressured by others to be something you're not? "Understand that although you have to play the game, you must say hello to *yourself* and see what *you* really want. Stand up for yourself, don't give up your real feelings to please others," is Diane's best advice.

Once you're in the game, there's still an incredible amount of competition, and not just for the juiciest roles. There's jockeying for fame, for who's on top today and who's comin' up fast behind you. If you look at show biz as a race, you're bound to lose. Your only competition should be yourself. You're the only one you should be trying to please.

THE SCHOOLWORK LOAD

A problem inherent to most teens in show biz is that of school. First of all, getting an education is a "job" in itself. Now you've got two jobs. After a long, tiring day on the set, adult performers go home and take a nice, long, relaxing bath. Teen actors go home to homework! Mr. Rock Star can go to a movie after hours in the recording studio. Ms. Teen Rock Star can go to her desk—and the algebra that awaits! It's easy to let your schoolwork slip, rationalizing, "What do I need algebra for? Or ancient history? I'll never need it. I *know* what my career is going to be and I'm getting on-the-job training." Don't buy into that line of thought—it's naive and seriously shortsighted. You must consider the possibility that show biz, for one reason or another, will not turn out to be your whole life. You need an education.

There's another, more immediate reason to keep up your grades, especially if you're working in California. You simply won't be allowed to continue acting if your grade in any subject slips below a C. You must maintain a decent average! Don't think exceptions are made, either. Corey Haim was cast in the TV series "Roomies," but when it was discovered he was failing history—he nearly got fired! Because Corey's a Canadian, he wasn't up on American history, so he had to take an intense course with a tutor to bring up his grade to stay on the show.

The law in California and many other states stipulates that you must have three hours of schooling each day. You work with a tutor, and, sometimes, if you're the only young person on a show or movie, it's a one-on-one situation. Most actors say they like this situation because they always understand things and they can move very fast on their work. Does it compensate for being away from a normal classroom, for missing out on the input of other kids and the social life that school provides? Everyone has his or her own answer to that one.

Your regular school is supposed to provide your assignments. It sounds reasonable, but it doesn't always work. Some schools just refuse to cooperate, and because of that many working teens have had to change from public to private schools. It may not make a difference when you're working, but when your work's over, it's tough getting used to a new school! Many celebs find they're better off in a private school where they're not the only ones working. Private schools tend to be more understanding about letting you off early for an audition or job.

Tommy Puett ("Life Goes On") went to a public school in his home town of Diamond Bar, California, about an hour's drive from Hollywood. Before he won the role on the series, he'd have to ask permission to leave early to go on auditions. His requests were not met with understanding. According to Tommy, some teachers, athletic coaches, and even guidance counselors were downright hostile. Tommy reveals, "They used to say to me, 'You think you're special, asking for special favors? You really think you're gonna make it in this business?' Clearly, they didn't! They used to call me Hollywood and they weren't saying it in a nice way."

THE UGLY GREEN MONSTER

Has it occurred to you that when you do start making it, people will be jealous? That takes a lot of performers by unhappy surprise, and there's not a young celeb in the business who hasn't faced it. Many people don't understand how hard you've worked and just think, "Oh, she got lucky." You may very well be treated differently at school. You may very well be accused of having changed, of being conceited and stuck-up. You may have trouble figuring out who your friends are. Some people, who may not have given you a toss before, will start being very friendly—others will avoid you like the plague!

Some kids are just jealous and will be envious of anything anyone else does, whether it's making the cheerleading squad or landing the lead in a TV series. It will help if you're aware of those feelings so you can fend off the ugly green monster. The consensus of advice is "the less you talk about your show biz successes the better. Answer questions as briefly as possible when you're asked, and don't offer information yourself. It will look like you're bragging, not sharing."

Tiffany always told kids at school she was baby-sitting when she was, in fact, recording her first album! "I didn't want them to feel that I was trying to say, 'Well, I'm better than you are,'" she explains. "Plus, I didn't want to say something and, then, not have it happen!" Which is excellent reasoning, especially in the topsy-turvy world of show biz! Any savvy insider will advise you not to tell people about auditions. If you don't get the job, you have to explain and that makes it worse. Also, don't flaunt it when you do land something. Few teenagers are going to be happy for you—they're not secure enough yet to feel anything but jealousy for you!

Jealousy can rear its ugly head within your family, too, and that's an even tougher reality. Being generous, making sure your brothers and sisters share in the excitement of your career, the successes as well as the failures, is one way of tempering it. Of course, in the best of situations, parents make the whole thing a family adventure, and make sure each child feels equally good about him or herself and has a dream to follow. Debbie Gibson's three sisters, all musicians, were never jealous of her success because they were each encouraged to develop their own talents. And they were supported in their dreams as much as Debbie was. Other teen stars have gladly paid for the college educations of their siblings and were supportive of everything they did.

Unfortunately, there are situations where the parents themselves are jealous. When a child is making more money than his or her dad, egos that are tied to financial success can't always handle it. Some families have broken up because of it. Most, however, find a way to deal with their problems and stay together.

FINDING TRUE FRIENDS

Dealing with friends can be tricky. It's best, most performers say, to stick with the ones "who knew you when"—the buddies who know you as a person, not as the star of a TV series! Jeremy Licht, who plays

Mark on "The Hogan Family," laughs when he tells about his friends coming to tapings of the show. "They sit in the audience and when I'm introduced and kids scream for me, they're always puzzled. They go, 'It's just Jeremy, why are you screaming?' It's important to me to have friends like that. They come to see me work, then we all go out together afterward and I'm just one of the guys."

You have to find your true friends, the celebs say, and stick with those you trust. They warn of "newfound friends" who might want to be around you because you're famous, not because they actually like you as a person. And when you go through a dry spell and aren't getting jobs, they'll drop you, count on it. And it will hurt!

A couple more pieces of advice from those who've been there. Don't give out your phone number to anyone you don't know very well, don't say where your school is, and never give out your address.

Having friends who are also in the business might seem like one way to avoid jealousy, but that's rarely the case. When all the teens you see are also performers, the tendency will be to talk shop all the time. Also it's a very gossipy (and sometimes mean-spirited) shop you're in! The buddy you're hanging with today is tomorrow's competition, and that's exactly the way many young performers see it.

A lot of young stars agree that having friends who are not in the business is a better idea. Kirk Cameron has almost no show biz friends and made a point of graduating from high school with his neighborhood friends in his regular class. Alyssa Milano says she has only one girlfriend—the teenager who lives across the street from her.

Tiffany has one best friend, too, a girl named Sunita who's not in show biz. One day the singer realized the importance of mutual support. "When I heard the song (about friendship) 'Wind Beneath My Wings,' I cried. I thought about Sunita and how it must be for her, hearing 'Tiffany, Tiffany, Tiffany' all day long— no one ever turning to her for an opinion or wanting to know if she's comfortable. So I make a point of doing that. She's one of the most important people in my life. She's a true friend who doesn't fawn all over me and tell me how wonderful I am. If I put on an outfit and ask her opinion, she'll often say, 'I think you should go change!' instead of complimenting me all the time."

INFLATED EGOS

That brings up an important point. It's easy to be dazzled, to believe the things that people in show biz start saying about you once you've made it. "There's no end to people telling you all day long how cute you are, how great you are, how talented you are," says actress Bobbi Ferguson, mother of up-and-coming star Jay Ferguson of the TV show "The Outsiders." "The trap is when you start believing it." Bobbi's advice to her son may sound harsh, but it goes a long way toward jolting a young, impressionable star back to reality. "Always remember," she says, "you are a product and somebody bought your product today. It has nothing to do with how special you are."

Having a distorted sense of yourself is a major pitfall for celebrity teens. You can—without even realizing it!—become conceited. Kirk Cameron's mom, Barbara, feels strongly that "It's very easy to get sucked in when everybody's pampering you, dressing you, doing your hair and makeup, getting things for you. And you're just standing there!" It's easy to feel that you're more important than the next guy when you're asked for autographs, when people scream for you, when you're mobbed after a show. That's a real trap, because as agent Judy Savage says, "When you're real high on the hog, you come down really fast!" No one's on top all the time, and picking yourself up once you're down is sometimes nearly impossible.

How to avoid the always-destructive ego problems, to separate the healthy ego you need to make it in this business from just plain conceit? "Treat it like a hobby you're lucky enough to get paid for," is Judy's best advice. "And never forget, even after you get a series or an Academy Award, you may never work again!" Understanding that will go a long way to keep your feet on the ground!

In all honesty, I've met *few* stars who haven't changed. I can't count the number of young, bright-eyed and incredibly nice teens starting out, who became obnoxious and self-important once fame hit. Those same performers, once their series got canceled, their movie or record got bombed, became remarkably humble once again. There are shining exceptions, of course, and the one who stands out most is Michael J. Fox. He never let dazzling fame go to his head. He never felt he was more important than the next guy and always understood he was doing a job and that his job depended on whether people were willing to pay money to see him!

But when your face is on the cover of teen magazines and journalists are lining up around the block to record your thoughts and opinions, it's hard to stay on the ground, to remember who you really are and where you come from. It's easy to come down with a bad case of "Hollywooditis," as agent Booh Schut puts it. In the worst case scenario it can be fatal.

THE ROOT OF ALL EVIL

There's no question that money can corrupt. A young person with access to a lot of it is an accident waiting to happen. For one thing, it tempts others to take advantage of you. For another, money can be so tied to ego and perceptions of worthiness that having a lot can make you feel important. It can even alter your relationship with your parents. I've heard of teen celebs who've become very disrespectful to their parents, who've actually said, "I pay your salary." Don't get the idea that most young stars have these disgusting thoughts. Most are well brought up, well grounded, and would be pulled out of the business for an improper remark like that. But it has happened.

The darkest side of all, naturally, is when money and a false sense of bravado lead to self-destructive behavior: namely, drugs and alcohol abuse. We've all heard some of the horror stories because a sensationalist press will always glory in playing them up. Nearly everyone who follows show biz knows that young Drew Barrymore had serious problems, as did Corey Haim and Corey Feldman. The history of young stars with "too much too soon" is there to be learned from.

161

GROWING INTO ADULT PERFORMERS

Another problem young stars face is when they're no longer young! The idea is to gracefully make the transition from teen performer to adult performer, but, traditionally, not many do. Reasons vary, of course. As you get older, deciding which roles to take or which songs to perform on an album gets trickier. A few bad decisions can kill a career, or, at least, put it on a long hiatus! Show biz is populated with teen idols who found themselves has-beens at the age of twenty-one! And that can be devastating.

Why do so many not make it? On an emotional level, many were not equipped. Vicki Light theorizes, "You have to be an adult, but you've never had a childhood. There was never any time to go through the normal, necessary steps. And many kid-turned-adult stars are secretly afraid they're going to get caught, discovered as a fraud. They never knew why they were successful when they were young. They're lacking in schooling, training, socialization skills, and educational background. It's no wonder they don't make it!"

If a long-term career is your goal, stay in school, get that education and get that training. In the long run, it'll serve you well.

COREY HAIM
How an Open Audition in Toronto Led to Hollywood Stardom!

"I'm from Toronto. My dad's a salesman and my mom's into computers, so they didn't know anything about show biz. Except my older sister, Carol, she was always interested. She's a really great actress, she used to win all these awards and things. It looked kinda cool to me, so I asked my parents if I could do some acting. A neighbor who lived across the street from school taught acting classes, so I went over there for a while.

"Then my mom heard about Faces and Places, a local commercials agency. Actually, it was the only one in Toronto. They took me on, and, mostly, I was modeling clothing for the Sears catalog. And I did this one commercial, for a furniture warehouse that went bankrupt!

"The agency also sent me up for a lead in a Canadian TV series called 'The Edison Twins,' and I got it. I played one of the twins.

"I'm not sure how this next thing happened exactly, but one day my mom came home and said we were

COREY HAIM

going to an audition for a movie, it was an open call. Since it meant I got out of a math test, it was okay with me.

"It was for the movie *Firstborn*. I lined up three different times with about forty other kids. Every time they'd go down the line and tell most of the other kids to go. They'd point to me and say, 'You. Stay.' I'd look behind me to make sure they meant me. And pretty soon it was between me and another kid. And I stayed. But I didn't actually have the part yet. They sent me to New York to screen-test. Then, I got it. I played the younger brother.

"The director of the movie, Stanley Jaffe, had a friend who was an agent in Hollywood, Vicki Light, and suggested she come up to Toronto and meet me. She met my whole family and I signed on with her agency.

"Things happened really fast after that. I filmed *Firstborn,* and then I just started landing parts in other movies. It was really like a fluke, the whole thing. I was having a great time, but I *was* really bummed about missing one whole year of hockey. But it never was a real conflict. I knew it was a choice, and I knew I was never going to be a professional hockey player anyway.

"Naturally, I stopped doing commercials. I like TV and movies the best. I've never done a play onstage. The theater's amazing, I mean you cannot mess up! That's the only problem, I don't like that. I don't want to be in front of three hundred people and forget a line, go blank!

"I guess most people know there have been some problems I've dealt with. At first, our whole family decided to move to California together, but it didn't work out. Carol went back to Canada and then my parents split up. That was real heavy.

"I got pretty messed up for a while. I was in with a bad crowd. I felt really bad about myself for a long time.

"But all that stuff is behind me now and I feel like I'm starting all over again. Things are good."

CHAPTER 11

THE PART YOUR PARENTS PLAY
(Read This Chapter with Mom and Dad!)

Back in the beginning of this book I said that if you're under eighteen, you can't hope to break in to show biz without the support of your parents. In this chapter, you're going to find out why.

Most likely, your folks fall into one of three groups: those who laugh off, or are pretty negative about your show biz dreams; those who push you into a career; and those who recognize that this is your dream and are completely supportive of it. Lucky you, if you're in the last group! You've already got a headstart on your way to a career in show biz.

PARENTS WHO DON'T—OR WON'T— OR CAN'T—TAKE YOU SERIOUSLY

Don't be discouraged if your folks don't take you seriously. Know that you're not alone. Most families do not want their kids in the business! They're not bad parents, they're not selfish parents—and they *do* understand a lot of things, probably more than you

167

realize. Parents who are negative about show biz may instinctively know how hard it is, how much rejection you'll face, how much time and effort it takes, and how the odds for a secure lifestyle are stacked against you. The whole idea may seem unrealistic to them, especially since they know how hard it is just to make a living in the "real world."

It might surprise you to know that many of the parents of the stars you know were pretty negative in the beginning too. Kirk and Candace Cameron's mom, Barbara, knew nothing about show biz and didn't think she was savvy enough to find out. Lin Milano had a promising career, which she understandably wasn't happy about putting on hold, when Alyssa began. The mother of New Kids on the Block's Jon and Jordan Knight had to be solidly convinced before she let her boys sign with a music manager. Trude Licht, Jeremy's mother, only let him get started when a friend convinced her that it might be the only way Jeremy would have enough money saved for college!

Marsha Hervey, Jason's mom, relates, "After I finally relented and let Jason do commercials, people would come up to me and say, 'How can you do this to your kid? How can you subject him to all this rejection?' I'd answer by saying that there's just as much rejection when kids choose up teams for a baseball game!"

Can you change your parents' minds? Should you even try? It depends on how strongly they object and how much you're willing to show them you're serious. But don't even try to convince them until you've accepted their point of view and taken some baby steps on your own. Be in your school plays; try out for the community theater roles; practice your singing and your instrument; prove that you're dedicated and committed. And keep your schoolwork up—the best way to show any parent how serious you are about anything is to start with good grades!

If, after everything you do, your parents are still opposed to your career, remember that most of today's biggest names were way past their teen years when they broke in. Look at some of the more established performers, like Tom Hanks, Michael Keaton, Meryl Streep, Billy Joel, and Elton John. They worked up to their success by taking small steps. They didn't hit Hollywood until they were out of their teens and didn't need to rely on their parents for help. Look how long they've lasted! Often, the longer it takes to make it, the longer a star stays on top of his craft. If show biz is your ambition for life, maybe it's not such a bad idea to wait until college or after to make it a reality.

PARENTS WHO PUSH TOO MUCH

Are you on the other end of the seesaw, a teen who's pursuing a show-biz career because mom or dad wants it for you? This situation is admittedly very tough to deal with. For clearly your parent doesn't see that you'd rather be reading, playing baseball, shopping, hanging out with your friends, or doing anything other than chase a dream.

What you have to do first is determine that you don't really want to do this. Next, you've got to sit down for a very serious talk with your mom and dad.

Do it at a time when they're not pressured or tired. Be rational and explain calmly that you don't want to go on another audition, that you don't want to be in the local play, or sing in front of an audience, or model for a clothing catalog. At some point, they should get and accept the picture.

Even if they don't, chances are, you won't get very far if the desire isn't yours. Agents, managers, and especially casting directors can tell—every time—if someone's being pushed into performing. Some managers and agents flatly refuse to even take on a client if they feel the parent is going to be trouble. Delores Robinson, a much-sought-after manager and the mother of Holly Robinson of "21 Jump Street," has seen too many "stage mothers." "Except in rare cases," she says, "I don't look to represent teenagers anymore—mainly because some parents are problems. The kids' hopes and dreams get all mixed up with the parents' hopes and dreams." Agent Booh Schut concurs: "If the motivation is from the parent, I can tell. I stay away from those situations. I can tell if the parents are living vicariously through their kids. It ends up changing them and their kids. It's not a pretty picture!"

PARENTS WHO ARE SUPPORTIVE— AND WHAT THEY DO

Are you one of the lucky ones with parents who are willing—even eager—to help? Count your blessings, for those parents are as rare as they are indispensable! Being a supportive parent of a teen who's trying to make it in show biz is a full-time job. There's no question about it. It takes an enormous amount of time, energy, effort, savvy, and money. It means sacrificing much of their time. They may even have to give up a paying job to help you. Tempestt Bledsoe's mom, Willa, had to give up her teaching job in Chicago when Tempestt landed "The Cosby Show" in New York. Not every parent who's willing to make those sacrifices, can!

What exactly is the job of the parent? The job description is lengthy—and varied! To start with, your parent has to act as a buffer between you and the adults in the world of show biz. Your parent usually makes the initial contacts with managers, agents, perhaps ad agency people, and sometimes casting directors.

When you're first starting out, a supportive parent might scour the newspapers for opportunities for you; make the hundreds of phone calls it takes to get going; help find the right agent; hire an attorney to look over any contract before it's signed; pick you up every day after school and drive you to lessons, interviews, and jobs; sit with you on those endless "waits"; lay out expenses; and keep detailed records.

Once you are starting to get established, the supportive parent must be with you on the set at all times, make provisions for the money you're earning, make sure the child labor laws are being obeyed, make sure you're being properly educated, and, most importantly, make sure you're protected.

Barbara Cameron expounds, "On the set, I'm there to make sure Candace and Kirk are always being treated as the professionals they are. Many directors and crew people look at them as just kids and don't take them seriously. It goes from blatant disregard of the hours they're supposed to be on the set to the hairdresser who may be pulling Candace's hair too tight. If she says it hurts, that her scalp is sensitive—I have to be there to make sure she's taken seriously and gets what she needs." When Barbara felt Candace's education was being compromised because the studio had hired one teacher for her *and* the younger cast members, the Camerons had that situation changed. Candace now has her own private tutor.

LIFTING YOU UP . . . AND BRINGING YOU BACK DOWN TO EARTH

The toughest part for a parent, perhaps, is bringing your spirits up when you're rejected—and bringing you back down to earth when your ego is perhaps soaring out of bounds! Whether you're just breaking in or somewhat established, you will face rejection at every turn. Staci Keanan's mom, Jackie Sagorsky, says, "I taught Staci never to feel that our lives depended on whether she booked a job or not. I also taught her never to feel any animosity toward the other kids up for the role. Our attitude always was 'if we get it, we get it, if we don't, we don't.'"

There may be times, too, when you *are* landing roles, and you might feel you're better than other kids because you're on TV or in a movie. It's the job of the supportive parent to bring you back to earth! In fact, it's when that aspect of support is missing that kids in show biz get into the most trouble!

The most level-headed parents make sure their

"celebrity children" aren't treated with undue deference. They insist their kids still do chores around the house and strive to teach them the value of money. Jeremy Licht's family did a superb job, as Jeremy explains: "I'd get an allowance and have to handle certain of my expenses. If my allowance money ran out before I was due for the next one, it was just too bad. I had to learn to make do without any money for a while—just like in real life! Now that I have my own apartment and am handling the rent, the electric bill and all the other bills, I see how important that training was."

Of course, as always, the best parents make sure their children's education remains the number-one priority in their lives.

HANDLING BROTHER AND SISTER

One of the touchiest problems supportive parents have to face is how the rest of the family deals with the success of the working teenager. No matter how many claim that their sisters and brothers aren't jealous, make no mistake about it, it's human nature to be envious. And the most candid families will reveal that it's true. Kirk Cameron's sister Bridgette was the one who really wanted to get into the business, and "it hurt" Barbara said, when she didn't. But like other healthy families, the Camerons found a way to deal with it. Many brothers and sisters of celebrities help out with the fan mail (and get paid for it!), get to travel to exciting places along with the working celeb, and get to experience, firsthand, a world they wouldn't know otherwise.

As you can see, supportive parents face complex challenges, and they give up a lot. Casting director Meg Liberman puts it most succinctly: "Mothers give up their lives!" If you've got that kind of mom, and a dad and family that supports her, cherish them all!

HOW POP PRINCESS DEBBIE GIBSON GOT GOING!

She burst onto the music charts when she was sixteen years old, but if there's an antithesis to an "overnight sensation," it's Debbie Gibson! The chart-topping teen had dreamed of rock 'n' roll stardom since the day she went to her first Billy Joel concert. She was only nine, but she knew music was her future. From that moment on she did everything in her power—and in her family's power—to make that dream come true.

In spite of her prodigious musical talent, intense ambition, and proximity to New York City (home was on nearby Long Island), Debbie ran up against every possible roadblock. Where other kids might have given up, Debbie drove on. In the end it was really her dedication and perseverance that got her across the finish line!

The third of four musically inclined sisters, Debbie began singing along with the radio as a tot and picking out tunes on the piano when she was only four. By five she was writing her own songs!

Encouraged by her family, Debbie trained hard.

DEBBIE GIBSON

SO YOU WANT TO BE A STAR!

She took years of piano lessons, plus dance, gymnastics, speech, acting, flute, and, of course, voice. Although the Gibsons had no show-biz connections or savvy about the entertainment world, they were behind Debbie one hundred and ten percent—more than most parents of talented kids. Debbie's dad changed positions at his airline job to have more flexibility in his schedule so he could drive Debbie to lessons, rehearsals, and auditions. Her mom took a secretarial job to help pay for all those lessons. Debbie's grandparents pitched in, too.

In addition to all her training, Debbie took every opportunity to perform. She appeared in all her school productions, in church, in regional theater on Sundays in a children's nightclub in New York City called Something Different, and even in the Metropolitan Opera's children's chorus. She also entered every talent contest she heard about.

Along the way, Debbie got turned down constantly. For every play she got, there were five she didn't get. She didn't even come in first in her school's talent show! She couldn't get an audition with the Metropolitan Opera until her piano teacher pulled some strings. It was only because a voice coach and piano arranger went to bat for her that she got to sing at Something Different.

Debbie got her first show-biz manager when her dance teacher's sister opened a management company. Debbie signed on and began auditioning for commercials. She went on interviews for two solid years before landing her first one. Eventually she made ten. She never did make it onto the TV show "Star Search," although she did get close two times.

Debbie took all the disappointments in stride. Of

course they hurt, but she didn't let the hurt stop her from trying.

Debbie continued to write songs and taught herself the rudiments of recording and set up a small at-home studio in order to get her songs on tape the way she heard them in her head.

She and her mom spent countless hours—and untold dollars!—sending out copies of Debbie's demo tapes to every record company in the New York phone book. But they knew no influential people, so it got them nowhere.

Finally, when she was thirteen, her third agent introduced her to a manager who did get her on track.

Debbie put her nose to the grindstone and turned out one fabulous demo tape after another. Eventually Atlantic Records gave her a shot, but the contract was for only *one* dance single! So even though she had that sought-after record contract, Debbie had to work even harder to prove herself. With her family behind her, Debbie did just that and made all her dreams come true.

Debbie Gibson's a bona fide star. She's recorded smash albums and won countless awards, but even that doesn't guarantee smooth sailing. The movie she's been trying to do, titled *Skirts,* has had problems getting off the ground. And then just when she finally thought all the deals were in place, the head of the movie studio resigned, and the new bosses weren't interested in *Skirts!*

Knowing Debbie, however, that won't stop her from making her movie—it may just take a little more time.

CHAPTER 12

YOU GOT THE PART!

Hooray for you! It's finally happened—you've landed your very first professional show-biz job! What exactly can you expect? What exactly will be expected of you? There's a great deal to cover, but most of the instructions you'll need involve the three *P*s— punctuality, preparedness, and professionalism.

Whether you're acting in a TV show, movie, or play, or singing and dancing onstage, if you're getting paid for it, you have entered the adult work force and will be expected to act like any other pro. Of course, your first few times are learning experiences, but, remember, the crew and other cast members are not there to teach you. It's your responsibility to pick up the pace of the place by yourself, through listening, observing, and following directions.

WHERE YOU GO

If you're doing a TV show or movie, you will have received your script ahead of time. Study all of it, not just your part, so you'll understand the total picture. That's part of preparedness.

You'll be assigned a certain day and time to report to the set or location. The show-biz term used is your "call time," which could be as early as six A.M. Teen performers often have to arrive earlier than the adults to get their required schooling in. Most TV shows and movies are taped or filmed at major studios or on locations in and around Los Angeles. That's where you'll be expected to report. In certain cases, this may mean relocating to Los Angeles temporarily. Of course, that depends on where you live and what sort of a part you've landed! If it's a regular on a series, you may have to live in an L.A. apartment for as long as the series is in production—at least six months for a successful show. Same with a movie role. You have to be within short commuting distance for however long it takes to shoot.

Once you and your parent or guardian have arrived at the studio, you'll be directed to the particular "stage" where your show or movie is being shot. Your stage will resemble all the others on the lot—a big, concrete, windowless building that looks rather like an old warehouse. All the stages are numbered and are the approximate size of a square city block.

WHAT IT'S LIKE

As you walk or drive through the lot to your stage, you may recognize lots of famous faces: Studios are where most of the well-known stars of TV shows and movies-in-progress spend their days. You'll see them walking to and from the stages, having lunch at the studio commissary (cafeteria), heading toward offices for meetings, or perhaps even shopping at the studio store. The temptation may be to stop a famous celeb and ask for an autograph. Know what? In most cases, that's perfectly okay—most celebs revel in recognition. Besides, now you're on their turf and likely to be seen as less a fan than a peer.

Your first stop will probably be at a trailer, that's used as a schoolroom, parked outside your stage. Your tutor will be there, so will any other youngsters in the cast. The three hours of school required aren't always consecutive. You may be in school for a half-hour, then called to the set to rehearse, then back to school. On certain days you may purposely do four or more hours. In show-biz terms that's called "banking" school hours so that on other, more important taping days, you're freer.

After school hours have been "logged" (yep, another term you'll hear on the set), you may be sent to "wardrobe," then, "hair and makeup." A professional hairdresser will fix your hair, and a makeup artist will size you up and decide what to apply. You may not have realized that teens on TV must wear makeup—actually, everyone does. This whole getting ready process may take several hours!

WHAT YOU DO

Finally, you're off to do your actual scenes. When you first walk onto the set, you may be in for a series of surprises. Inside, the stages don't look much better than on the outside! They still look like huge, dusty warehouses, albeit crowded with huge rolling cameras, thick cable lines all over the floor, rows of track lights hanging down from the ceiling, and three-sided "rooms" that are the actual sets.

There are lots of casually dressed crew people around—could be up to twenty-five of them—and for the most part, it doesn't actually look like anyone's working! Don't be fooled. Putting a TV show or movie together requires a lot of unseen work by a host of technical folks who set the stage before the performers come in. It takes time for the camera operators, sound and lighting technicians, prop masters, script and continuity people to get ready for each scene. Often, there are many changes before the director is ultimately satisfied with the set.

During this time, actors wait around. "Hurry up and wait" is a show-biz saying. Yes, *you* must be punctual, ready, and available when your name is called, but there's a great deal of "downtime" for just hanging around and waiting to be called. Some young actors use this time to do homework, phone friends, or study their scripts.

Dressing rooms may be another surprise if you expected glamour. On most television shows, the dressing rooms are tiny, cramped little boxes in the far reaches of the stage. They do have the actor's name on the door. If you're not a regular on the show, you may be assigned one that simply says "Guest" on it; you may also be sharing it with other guests! On some movies and other TV shows, the actors do get Winnebago-like trailers for private dressing rooms and they are much nicer!

As a newcomer, however, it's better for you to stay on the set than head for a dressing room. Observe all that's going on. "Downtime" is the perfect time to ask questions about anything you don't understand, from terminology to who does what on the show! Learning as much as you possibly can is part of what professionalism is all about.

The person who really runs the show on the set is the director; helping him or her are several ADs, or assistant directors. The ADs are the ones who'll be working with you most directly. You should turn to them for advice and listen for them to call you. Be there when you're called—the first time—and be ready to perform. Know that if you're not on time and ready to go, you may get a reputation for being difficult. And that means it will be difficult to get another job. Directors are well aware that there are one hundred other teens just like you looking for a break. Replacing a difficult teen is easy.

You may not think you're being difficult, just because you were chatting and didn't hear your name called. But that may be all it takes. For there are some directors who are harder on kids. Remember, it's not their job to train you. You're expected to come in, know exactly what you're supposed to do, and do it, with a minimum of fuss. Welcome to the real world!

Knowing your lines and cues is a major part of preparedness. Naturally, you've worked on your scenes beforehand, either on your own or with a coach or manager. Every performer has a favorite method for memorizing lines. Some TV actors do the bulk of memorizing lines during rehearsals. They focus on an object in the room and that triggers the line they're to say during that scene. "My Two Dads" star Staci Keanan usually just reads the script "again and again and again until I know my lines and my cues." Others learn it a page at a time, testing themselves on each page before going on to the next. Actor Wil Wheaton doesn't like to put in too much prep time. He's a quick study who can read, interpret, and memorize easily. Wil feels that too much memorizing beforehand ruins the spontaneity of a scene. By this time, you should have a method that works for you.

Rehearsal is the time you practice with the other actors. For a half-hour TV comedy, like "Growing Pains," "Who's the Boss?" or "Full House," rehearsals take about four days. On the fifth, the actual show is taped, usually twice in the same day, and often before a live studio audience. That can be fun or downright scary for the newcomer! Yes, there have been times when young actors have "freaked out" on tape days. One little girl who was the lead in a series got so scared, she cried. She was replaced the next day. Understand that it is an intimidating situation, but if you're trained, if you're comfortable around adults, if you know what's going on and what you're doing, you won't freak out. You'll be just fine!

Shows like "21 Jump Street," "Doogie Howser, M.D.," "The Wonder Years," or a miniseries, TV movie, or feature film work a little differently. They rehearse and shoot actual footage each day. They take longer to complete each episode, often seven or eight working days as opposed to five.

At some point in each working day, there's an hour set aside for lunch, which the actors usually take with the crew, either at the commissary or right on the stage where a catered lunch is available.

After lunch it's back to work—and more waiting! Indisputably, the people who do the most waiting around, however, are the parents or guardians hired to be with you. Many use the time to read, knit, or work on some quiet, solitary project, while keeping at least one eye on you!

ACTION!

During rehearsals, outside noises and distractions (chatting, jangling jewelry) are tolerated, but every once in a while you hear the words, "Quiet! Rolling!" followed quickly by "Action!" Yes, there is a black clapboard slate that's snapped before each "take" of each scene. At the moment the cameras are rolling, you're doing the real performing and any errant sound, any ringing phone or closing door, will be picked up by the sound technician and the scene will be ruined. That, however, is only one reason why the same scene may be reshot many—sometimes twenty or more!—times. It happens more often in a one-hour show or movie than in a sitcom, and it happens for any number of reasons. Actors flub their lines all the time, directors decide someone should be standing here instead of there or that someone should enter from this angle rather than that. Or there may be no reason you can figure out. Some directors just like doing things over and over again!

Be prepared to repeat your scene many times; often the hairdresser or makeup person will be called onto the set to freshen up the actors. Repeating scenes is a major, but necessary, time consumer. On the movie *The Outsiders* there was a scene where young Tommy Howell was pushed into a wading pool. Each time it was reshot, Tommy had to dry off, change clothes, and have his hair blown dry. That scene, thirty seconds on the screen, took three days to shoot. (I know, I was there.) Similarly, a "21 Jump Street" scene where Johnny Depp got in and out of a car in the rain (ten seconds on TV) took a full day to complete. A simple scene that requires two actors to walk from one spot to another and deliver two lines can—and usually does—take all morning.

This is not glamorous! This is downright boring—unless, that is, you make it a learning experience. Seek to understand the reasons for all the retakes. The more you know, the better off you are. Not many young performers bother to learn all they can on the set. This will give you a distinct advantage over the competition. The more you understand, the more professional you can be. When directors see that you're taking the job seriously, that you're interested, you may be rehired more often than not. It's just as easy to get a good reputation as a bad one!

At the end of the day you're dismissed and given your "call sheet" for the next day. All the actors' "call times" are listed as well as where to show up and what the director plans to accomplish that day.

Unless you're the star of the show, in almost no case will you be required to be on the set every day. You only come when your scenes are being rehearsed or shot. Since the schedule changes daily, it requires a lot of flexibility on your part and on your family's part! Because you're not on the set every day—unless it's a sitcom where you're there on the days they tape—you don't get to see the final show until it airs or is ready to be screened. Sometimes, you have no idea how a movie's going to turn out. They're most often filmed out of sequence! You may be as surprised as the general public.

SO YOU WANT TO BE A STAR!

Whatever you do, don't forget to get a videotape of your work, or of the entire show or movie. You always need samples of you in action!

When a project is finished, especially if it's a movie, there's often a "wrap" party to which all the cast and crew are invited. TV series customarily have their parties at the end of each season. That's the place where you may, finally, find some glamour. Wrap parties are where you socialize, eat, and, most importantly, make contacts for your *next* big acting job!

JASON HERVEY
 A "Wonder Years" Star
Shares His Experiences

"I grew up in show business, it's been my life. I don't know anything different! I was this chubby-cheeked, funny-looking little kid. My mom says I looked like a potato, I'd walk in a room and people would just laugh. I was funny, I was wild, I was totally outgoing, I never wanted to go to sleep!

"My mom's brother was—is, actually—a business manager for celebrities. He had a client, a friend of ours who's an actor. And this friend had been bugging my mom since I was two, that I should be in this business. So when I was four, my mom finally took me to his agent, Beverly Hecht. And she loved me, my mom says, because I had 'a look and a mouth'—you never knew what was going to come out of it!

"So I started working and I didn't think anything of it. My very first job was a commercial for Del Monte ketchup, but it only ran in Japan. When I got to be school age, I liked getting out of school to go to work. I never had a problem with auditions, they were kind of fun, whether I got the job or not. I'd see the same kids on auditions all the time and it got to be like our little

188

JASON HERVEY

group. Wil Wheaton used to bring his cars and we'd all play in the waiting room, me, Wil, Kirk Cameron, Scott Grimes, Alyssa Milano.

"When I was about seven, I think it was Henry Winkler who suggested to my mom that I get some training. So I took some classes with Virgil Frye, he's Soleil Moon Frye's dad and he runs an acting school. Then, later on, I studied with Ernie Lively, whose kids Robin and Jason are actors, too.

"I did a lot of commercials—my mom, who keeps track, says it was like two-hundred-fifty! Because I was so unusual-looking and so uninhibited—I am the type of person who cannot be embarrassed!—I got one out of every four I went for. I also did lots of voiceovers and some short-lived series before 'The Wonder Years.' I was in a couple of movies, too.

"Except for one time at a theater in Los Angeles, I haven't done any plays. And it's funny, because Dan Lauria, who plays the dad in 'The Wonder Years,' is an accomplished stage actor. And he tells me and Fred that we're not really actors. Until you've done stage work, he says, you can't call yourself an actor. He says Fred and I are TV stars, not actors. But he says it with affection, so it's okay.

"I never let rejection bother me. I'd go on an interview and then just forget about it. I'd come home and play street hockey or football on the lawn.

"I don't feel I missed out on anything, growing up in the business. I played soccer, I was on the swim team, I went to the Y, I skateboarded, I went to Hebrew School and studied for my Bar Mitzvah for four years. If anything, show biz was the least important part of my life.

"I'm not saying I didn't make any sacrifices. Some

days, when I went on two or three auditions after school, I did miss some things. But what I was doing was so rewarding, so fulfilling. Now I'm eighteen and I don't care what I have to give up to do this. I like working, I like being independent, not having to ask my parents for money.

"Speaking of parents, I was always lucky that mine supported me totally. But they would have supported me in anything. If I said I wanted to leave the business tomorrow, they'd say, 'Good, Jason. We'll support you.' You do need your parents to make it in this business. I wouldn't suggest trying without them. If they don't understand how important this is to you, try and tell them that it really means the world to you.

"But don't get into it for the money. Do it for love, because you have a passion, a flair, a desire to perform in front of people. You gotta have so much strength within yourself to not care if you don't get something, to keep goin', to hold your head up and tell yourself, 'Next time, I'm gonna knock it out of the park!' You've gotta be a strong person, 'cause this business is so fickle."

CHAPTER 13

GET GOING NOW!

Can't wait to get going? Desperate to be discovered? You know by now that it won't be easy, but opportunities are there. Yes, even in your city or town—if you know where to look for them!

There are performing jobs to be had right in your hometown, courtesy of your local and cable TV channels, as well as local radio stations. *Local TV stations* are those other than the three big network affiliates, ABC, CBS, and NBC. Usually, they have offices right in your nearest small city and are pretty easy to locate. Check the phone book or call Information. These stations run commercials for local businesses, and they almost always use local talent. Spend some time watching the commercials on those stations, see if anyone in your age range is represented in the ads. If they do use teens, call the station, ask for their advertising department and find out where they get their performers. They may direct you to an agency—it may be a modeling agency. Although you may choose not to sign on with the particular agency, at least you'll know its clients do get legitimate, albeit local, TV work. Before you sign up for any work, of course, make sure you and your parents understand the terms of your employment. Find out in advance what you'll be expected to do, what the compensation is and get it in writing. Check with the Better Business Bureau first.

Nearly every town has a *cable TV* franchise, and if you check out not only the commercials but also the programming on cable, you may see teen performers. Once again, find the phone number, call and see what opportunities exist. With a small local cable franchise, there's less chance of getting paid for what you do, but there is experience to be gained.

Local radio stations hire young people for their commercials. Call up and find out where they get their voiceover performers; they may send you to an agency, or they may have a more direct way for you to apply. You never know until you try!

Local TV and radio stations may also have *internship opportunities* available that you may want to look into for the summer. You wouldn't get paid and you may not be involved in any sort of entertainment, but you would get a feel for the whole radio or TV scene.

Also try your state's Film Commission, which has information on movies being filmed in your area. Every state has at least one film commission, bigger states like New York, California, Texas, and Florida have several. Canada has its own film commission with information on productions in each province. Contact them in writing and ask who handles the hiring of "extras" for the movies. Extras, or atmosphere people, are the faces you see in the background of movies and TV shows; they have no lines and most viewers hardly notice them, but they are needed in all productions to make them look realistic. No one suggests that becoming an extra is a way of getting discovered, but it can be a way to get your feet wet and see what movie-making's all about!

THEME PARK POSSIBILITIES

If you've ever visited a theme or amusement park, you know that, in addition to all the rides, most of the big ones offer a variety of productions that showcase singers, dancers, actors, and musicians. Ever thought about the entertainers who appear in these shows? Just like you, they're aspiring professionals! In fact, theme parks are the largest employers of young talent in the country. Chances are, you will not be magically discovered while whooping it up in the Hoop De Do Revue, but you will be gaining good experience, making money, having fun, and meeting people with similar aspirations. Before Patrick Swayze became everyone's favorite *Dirty Dancer,* he spent one summer in a theme park as Prince Charming in a production of *Snow White!*

Here are some of the major theme parks in the U.S.A. and how you contact them.

The **Walt Disney Theme Parks,** including **Disneyland** in California, **Disney World, Epcot** and **MGM Disney Studios** in Florida offer a wide range of entertainment opportunities. They employ hundreds of full-time entertainers and hold open auditions in cities all over the country. You do need to be eighteen years old or over for most of the performance jobs, but there are opportunities for younger teens in other, more peripheral, positions in parades and as Disney characters. Disney World also offers specific college band and orchestra jobs for which you get academic credit.

The way to find out about auditions for any entertainment job in the Disney organization is to write to either: **Disney Auditions, P.O. Box 10000, Lake Buena Vista, FL 32830-1000,** or **Disneyland, Entertainment Division, Work Experience Program, 1313 Harbor Blvd., Anaheim, CA 92803.** Send a self-addressed, stamped envelope and ask to be put on the mailing list for audition information. They should be able to send a very complete list of exactly who may audition, when, and where, what positions are available, how the pay scale and benefits work, and what the requirements are.

The **Six Flags Organization** operates seven theme parks and offers performance jobs for young entertainers, ages sixteen to twenty-five. You can contact an independent producer for information about auditions. That address is **GP Show Productions, 1912 E. Randol Mill Road, Suite 311, Arlington, TX 76011.** Send a photo and resume with detailed info about your experience, skills, and training. If possible, send an audio or videotape of your work. Let them know which of the Six Flags park you live nearest.

Or, you may contact the Six Flags Show Productions central office. Submit your resume and photo by November for their traditional January–April auditions which are held in the cities which house the parks. The central address is: **Six Flags Show Productions, 1168 113th Street, Grand Prairie, TX 75050.**

Of course, you can write to each of the Six Flags Amusement Parks individually. In each case, send

your inquiry to the attention of: **Show Operations.**
Individual addresses are: Six Flags Great Adventure,
P.O. Box 120, Jackson, NJ, 08527; Six Flags Magic
Mountain, P.O. Box 5500, Valencia, CA 91355; Six
Flags Over Georgia, P.O. Box 43187, Mabelton, GA
30378; Six Flags Astro World, 9001 Kirby Drive,
Houston, TX 77054; Six Flags Great America, P.O.
Box 1776, Gurnee, IL 60031; Six Flags Over Mid-
America, P.O. Box 666, Eureka, MS 63025; Six Flags
Over Texas, P.O. Box 191, Arlington, TX 77004-0191.

Busch Gardens is another major theme park operator with opportunities for entertainment employment. There are three parks to consider. Busch Gardens Tampa/The Dark Continent has openings for
actors, singers, mimes, musicians, comedians, and
more. You need to be at least eighteen years old. For
specific audition info, contact **Deborah Baker, Audi-**
tion Coordinator, Busch Gardens Tampa, 3605
Bougainvillea Ave., Tampa, FL 33612.

Busch Gardens/The Old Country has similar openings and requirements. Write for audition information to: **Busch Gardens/The Old Country, Live**
Entertainment Audition Coordinator, One Busch Gar-
dens Blvd., C8785, Williamsburg, VA 23187-8785.

Sesame Place is also part of the Busch Gardens
organization. Sesame Place hires actors, dancers, musicians, and strolling entertainers. You must be sixteen years old to apply. Write: **Sesame Place, Live**
Entertainment, 100 Sesame Place Road, Box 579,
Langhorne, PA 19047.

An independent producer who puts together shows
for **Hershey Park** in Hershey, Pennsylvania, and **Ac-**
tion Park in McAfee, New Jersey, is **Allan Albert, Inc.**

at **561 Broadway, Suite 10C, New York, NY 10012.** They're looking for singers, dancers, actors, musicians, clowns, and mimes. You must be a high school graduate or older.

Dollywood is the theme park owned by entertainer Dolly Parton. To find out about who they hire for entertainment, write: **Dollywood, 700 Dollywood Lane, Pidgeon Forge, TN 37863.**

Cedar Point/The Amusement Park features four theaters and looks for musicians, singers, and dancers over the age of eighteen. Write: **Cedar Point/The Amusement Park, CN 5006, Sandusky, OH 44870.**

There are other smaller theme parks all over the U.S.A. and Canada, too, that may be worth contacting. But before you get involved with any of them, be sure to investigate first. You really will have to be a detective, find out the names of some teens who've performed at these parks and ask for their advice and recommendations.

TALENT CONTESTS

Along with the jobs you can get now, there are other possibilities to explore. Talent contests are held all over the globe. If you're really serious about getting discovered, you'll find out where they are in your area and sign up! Don't forget that you may have to pay an entrance fee to compete, and not all talent contests are worth it.

Debbie Gibson entered every single one she could find, from the time she was six years old! She sang, played piano, and wrote a patriotic song for a radio contest. You name it, she entered it! There wasn't one single contest that led directly to stardom, but they did net her contacts in the entertainment industry—and they led to stardom!

Beauty pageants may look like an obvious route to show biz, but nearly every single professional in the entertainment industry will tell you that they are not. With one or two exceptions (singer Vanessa Williams, who was Miss America, and actress Renee Jones on "L.A. Law") hardly any popular celebs got started that way. If that's a route open to you, however, and it doesn't cost anything, you may want to enter, just for the experience. But don't enter thinking it'll lead to a show-biz career.

One talent contest that very well may be a direct route to stardom, however, is the TV show "Star Search." That popular show gives aspiring entertainers a shot at national exposure and the chance to win big money. Stars you know who've appeared on the show before they were famous include Tiffany, The Boys, Ami Dolenz, and Sinbad from the TV show "A Different World." "Star Search" is open to teen singers and rock bands, and it has specific procedures for auditioning. Before you do, however, note that according to talent manager Maralyn Fisher, "'Star Search' is *not* for rank amateurs, you should be relatively accomplished before you apply." Applying, however, is a relatively simple procedure. Send a tape, audio or video, of yourself singing, dancing, or playing in your band to "Star Search," **875 Third Avenue, New York, NY 10022.** Singers should choose a couple of songs, in different styles. A tip: don't sing Debbie Gibson, Tiffany, Whitney Houston, or Bobby Brown tunes. The "Star Search" staff has been deluged with those! Do something different!

SO YOU WANT TO BE A STAR!

Along with the tape, send your photo (it can be a snapshot, but it should show what you look like!) and resume listing *any* experience you've had, even school plays. Include your name and parent's work phone number on every single item you send.

Maralyn's "Star Search" staff reviews all submissions. They only contact the applicants they want to audition in person, however. Auditions are held at different times of the year in several cities. If they want to see you, they'll notify you with all the pertinent details. Maralyn warns, however, that there are "phony 'Star Searchers' out there, who *charge* for auditions, so beware! Anyone that approaches you on the street and says he's from 'Star Search' and wants to charge you money is a phony. That is not the way we go about finding new talent. You apply to us. We contact you if we're interested. You never pay to audition."

JOHNNY DEPP'S JOURNEY TO TV AND MOVIE STARDOM

Johnny was a little boy from a small town in Florida whose love of music led to stardom as an actor. He had no show-biz connections, no money, and very little family support, for he came from a broken home.

Johnny's love of music started in church, when he'd listen to his Uncle Denny's gospel group. He got his first guitar when he was twelve, and locked himself in his bedroom after school every day until he taught himself how to play! There was no money for lessons, and by his early teens Johnny had a dream to make it as a rock star!

He began by forming little bands with his junior high school cohorts and playing with them wherever they could. "We'd play at parties in people's backyards," he remembers. "At school dances and bonfires. We'd keep getting better." Johnny began writing songs, too, although he didn't get much of a chance to perform his originals; mostly, all the bands he was with sang covers of popular songs.

Johnny was part of his school's band and performed

JOHNNY DEPP

in its annual Friendship Train musical. Eventually, however, the combination of family problems (his parents divorced) and his own troubled teen years led him to drop out of high school. He regretted the move and even tried to re-enroll. "But they wouldn't let me," he admits. "The dean at the time just basically told me that my heart wasn't in it. I should follow my dream, which was music."

That's exactly what he did. Taking a job in construction to earn money, the sixteen-year-old jumped into several different bands and spent his evenings playing in seedy clubs throughout south Florida. When he was eighteen, he joined a band called The Kids, which had a reputation as one of the area's best local groups. The Kids felt they had a shot at rock stardom and worked hard to make their dream come true. They even released, at their own expense, an independently produced single. It got some airplay on local public radio, but it didn't get them the record contract they hoped for.

At the end of 1983 The Kids decided to go to California, feeling their chances of success were better there. With no money and no show-biz connections, Johnny went along with the band. That was when the hard times really began! For The Kids had trouble getting gigs and all the guys took menial jobs just to make ends meet. Among other things, Johnny sold pens over the phone!

He did make friends in Hollywood and one of them, luckily, was the actor Nicolas Cage, director Francis Ford Coppola's nephew, who had a lot of connections. Nick thought Johnny would make a great actor and insisted he meet with an agent.

A skeptical Johnny Depp did just that, and before

he knew it, he was cast, without an ounce of training, in his first movie, *A Nightmare on Elm Street*. Johnny's incredible looks and his natural presence impressed not only that agent but also the casting director of the movie, the director, and, most importantly perhaps, the director's teenage daughter and her friends!

That movie led to others, including the Academy Award–winning *Platoon* and, of course, a starring role in "21 Jump Street." Now Johnny can just about write his own ticket in show biz—and he has, opting for offbeat movies like *Cry-baby* and *Edward Scissorhands*. Maybe one day he'll even get back to his beloved music.

There's no question that Johnny Depp's a natural, and he'll be the first to admit that he "fell into" acting stardom. But he did pay his dues, albeit as a struggling musician, and he hasn't escaped the perils of fame, including loss of privacy and problems with a prying press.

Through it all, Johnny's always remembered the advice he got from his parents: "Don't give in to something if you don't believe in it. Stick with what you believe in and go with that. Always, follow your heart."

CHAPTER 14

RESOURCES

THE SHOW BUSINESS UNIONS

These unions have regional branches in most states. Write to the main offices (I've listed main offices on both coasts) and ask for the branch nearest you. Your branch office should be able to provide you with a sample contract and a list of franchised agents (for a nominal fee and a business-size self-addressed, stamped envelope). SAG may also have a Parent's Pack available, which provides materials for someone under eighteen joining the union.

The Screen Actor's Guild (SAG)
7065 Hollywood Blvd.
Hollywood, CA 90028

The Screen Actor's Guild
1515 Broadway
New York, NY 10036

American Federation of Television and Radio Artists (AFTRA)
6922 Hollywood Blvd.
8th floor
Hollywood, CA 90028

RESOURCES

American Federation of Television and Radio Artists
260 Madison Ave.
New York, NY 10016

Actor's Equity Association (AEA or EQUITY)
165 W. 46th Street
New York, NY 10036

Actor's Equity Association
6430 Sunset Blvd.
Suite 1002
Hollywood, CA 90028

Alliance of Canadian Cinema, TV and Radio Artists
(ACTRA)
Suite 911
525 Seymour Street
Vancouver, BC
V6B 3H7, Canada

Alliance of Canadian Cinema, TV and Radio Artists
2239 Yonge Street
Toronto, ONT
M4S 2B5, Canada

BOOKS, MAGAZINES, AND
TRADE PUBLICATIONS

Reading up on show biz is always a good idea, and the following materials will give you great advice as well as wonderful leads. Some you may find in special drama bookshops, for others you will have to write to the publisher for information. I've listed addresses—write first and ask about ordering information before you send any money.

RESOURCES

Summer Theatre Directory
Regional Theatre Directory
Directory of Theatre Training Programs
(all) by Jill Charles
Write for price info: Theatre Directories, P.O. Box
519, Dorset, VT 05251

Summer Theater Guide from an Actor's Viewpoint
Regional and Dinner Theater Guide from an Actor's
Viewpoint
(both) by John Allen
P.O. Box 2129, New York, NY 10185

The Professional Theater Guide for the U.S.
Ra-Mos Publications
P.O. Box 46423
Los Angeles, CA 90046
(Only available through the mail.)

The Backstage Handbook for Performing Artists
by Sherry Eaker
Backstage Publications, Inc.
330 W. 42nd Street
New York, NY 10036

The Informed Performer's Directory of Instruction for
the Performing Arts
by Kat Smith
Avon Books

Kid Biz
by Nancy Carson and Allen Fawcett
Warner Books

How to Be a Working Actor
by Mari Lyn Henry and Lynne Rogers
M. Evans & Co., New York

RESOURCES

TRADE PUBLICATIONS

These newspapers are hard to find on the news-stands in most areas; if you want access to them, you'll have to subscribe. Write first and ask about subscription information. They're all chock-a-block with show-biz news, and often there are audition notices posted.

Backstage
330 W. 42nd Street
New York, NY 10036

Drama Logue
P.O. Box 38771
Los Angeles, CA 90038

Variety (Weekly)
475 Park Ave. South
New York, NY 10016

State Film Commissions Directory
Locations Magazine
Association of Film Commissions, Int.
c/o The Wyoming Film Office
I-25 and College Drive
Cheyenne, WY 82002

SPECIALTY BOOKSTORES

If you can't find the books you want, these theatrical bookstores have catalogs you can buy listing all their books.

Applause Books
211 W. 71st Street
New York, NY 10023

Samuel French's Theater & Film Bookshop
1-800-8-ACT NOW
or write: 7623 Sunset Blvd., Los Angeles, CA 90046

About the Author

Randi Reisfeld is editorial director of *16* magazine, a youth-oriented entertainment publication. She has interviewed and written about scores of young celebrities. In addition, her work includes biographies of actor Johnny Depp and singer Debbie Gibson. Her articles have appeared in *The New York Times, Scholastic, Little League,* and *Women's World* magazines.

She resides in the New York area. And, yes, she, too, at one time, wanted to be a star. If she only knew then, what she knows now!